Searching for Nausicaa

Short Stories by Alexis Levitin

OPEN ENDS PRESS

Cover and interior design by Mark Revis
Cover photo: Naxos

This is the first paperback edition.

ISBN: 979-8-9940326-0-2
Manufactured in the United States

Table of Contents

Searching For Nausicaa..................................5

Intragalactic Chess Encounter............................ 13

Love 25

If Only I Could........................35

Joy........................43

Calypso........................55

How Sad the Flesh........................63

Till it's Gone........................73

Last Love 81

Centerfold........................89

Do You Think He Loves Me?........................97

Simply Revenge........................ 103

Beneath the Bougainvillea of Folegandros........112

Chess on Naxos 117

Sagres........................121

Norwegian Butterfly........................ 129

Melú........................133

Death by Drowning........................ 139

Kindness 147

Autumnal Love 159

In the Year of the Plague, 2020 165

A Touch of Unexpected Grace........................173

Acknowledgements........................181

About the Author........................ 182

She cannot fade, though thou hast not thy bliss,

For ever wilt thou love, and she be fair!

– John Keats

SEARCHING FOR NAUSICAA

Historians disagree. So, too, studious classicists, inventive mythologists. Consensus has proven impossible. No one can convince anyone else of their own certainty. Some maintain her kingdom was on Kerkyra. Others say not at all; clearly, her people were from the ancient land of Crete. Some researchers in the recondite find the preponderance of evidence suggesting the fabled island of Atlantis as her true abode. But whatever researchers and savants said, wherever Jim went amongst the endless archipelagos of Greece, he always searched for her. He doubted she would be on Naxos, but what could he do? Since he was there, he had to look for long-lost Nausicaa there.

At the beginning of this journey, he had foolishly stopped off at Aegina, eager to set foot on an island as soon as possible. It had been several years since his last visit to Greece. On Aegina, despite the small island's unromantic aspect, he had, indeed, met a lovely young Greek creature, the right age for Nausicaa. But her name was Alexandra, and she looked wildly modern, like an innocent version of Madonna, if such a thing could be imagined. He was touched by her directness, her lack of guile, her unawareness of her own childlike beauty. Her father owned the restaurant where they met, and Jim happily stayed to eat a fine dinner of skewered lamb, rice, a feta salad, and honey-covered baklava, accompanied by the usual retsina. But the next day, since she was not Nausicaa, he said goodbye and continued on his way.

The ferry stopped at Milos, but he couldn't bear the thought of spending time on that unfortunate island, whose entire male population had been slaughtered in a punitive raid by Athens when they refused, quite reasonably, to take sides in the war between that noble beacon of democracy and Sparta. A moral low point from which the Athenian Polis never recovered. After another two or three stops, the ferry came to Folegandros, and there he alighted to try his luck.

He had searched the island far and wide without success. But in an ordinary white-washed restaurant in a square at the heart of the Chora, he had, in fact, come upon a green-eyed beauty deeply absorbed in a movie magazine and nibbling on olives and dolmades. He had had his doubts, of course, but had dared to strike up an awkward conversation, just to make sure. A bit impatient at being torn away from her celebrities and their woes, she did, at least, reveal her name. "Angeliki," she said, impatient to return to the glorious lives of others. Lovely to look upon, but far from a Nausicaa, as he had surmised from the first. He ordered two ouzos, clinked glasses with her, said *yassou*, and gulped his down. Then, with a half-hearted smile, he took his leave. Still sipping her ouzo, she looked rather relieved that he was moving on. In fact, they were both relieved. And so he boarded the lumbering ferry to make his way to yet another island. Another hope.

Of course, he had combed the length of Amorgos before coming to Naxos. The island was long, relatively untouched by tourism, with no spectacular beaches, but with many whitewashed mountain villages scattered along the island's spine. So undisturbed was Amorgos that had Nausicaa wished to remain incognito forever, that would have been a sly and clever choice. On the other hand, would any Nausicaa, even today, armed with Netflix, C-Span, and an iPhone, tolerate living at such a far remove from the nearest beach? Quite unlikely. He was not surprised, then, to find no trace of her in those quiet, unassuming clusters of houses, etched sharp beneath the Mediterranean sun, like scattered pulsing shards from a shattered mirror.

His general practice remained the same. Whatever island he disembarked upon, he would quickly rent a scooter, buy the best map available, and putter along to the most distant outposts, the furthest promontories of land. His habit was always to follow the least traveled road or track to its very end. Sometimes a path would peter out in the middle of nowhere, degenerating into a narrow goat path, wending its way through the thistles, and he would simply return the way he had come. Sometimes a path would lead him to a small, deserted beach. There he might stop, take a swim, carefully avoiding the pink jellyfish that had somehow discovered paradise, lie in the warm sun for an hour or so, then return to his search. But nowhere had he ever met Nausicaa, not on any of the countless islands he had visited.

And now Jim had come to Naxos, where the results of his search, at least so far, were no different from the results encountered on all the other islands. But he simply kept on. He loved the harsh sound of the cicadas in the noonday heat, and he loved the smell of oregano and thyme coming from the desiccated dusty brush. The road he was following today had not shrunk into a path, as so often happened. It had maintained its dimensions and was lined with bits of plastic caught on the spiny underbrush on either side, with occasional slabs of cardboard littering the roadway. How untidy the inhabitants of paradise could be, he mused.

When he saw plumes of smoke ahead, he wondered if he was coming to a village, though none was noted on his map. As the road kept climbing, he found himself rolling round a broad curve. Suddenly, his way was blocked. There in the middle of the track stood three healthy goats, staring at him through imperturbable, opaque yellow eyes. The biggest, armed with a baronial spread of horns, wore an impeccable burnt sienna coat and a long, wispy beard. He looked like a scientist or a Buddhist monk, inscrutable. His gaze was both stern and distant, as if the interloper on a scooter, though clothed in substance, was a figure of no importance in the universe. The others also stared at him, but then, satisfied with his insignificance, returned to snuffing and browsing amongst the debris lining the roadway.

Wheeling carefully between them, he came to the end of the road, and there his destination revealed itself. There was no mountain village harboring, in the gentle shade beneath trellised bougainvillea, the Nausicaa of his dreams. Instead, there lay before him a huge pit, as if at the end of the world. And it was filled with mounds of construction debris, broken drywall, shattered glass, trash bags filled with discarded school assignments and last week's bureaucratic paperwork, and everywhere, odorous piles of everyone's daily garbage. It was the island dump, unmarked on any map, with crows and seagulls wrangling for the choicest items. Everywhere lay fragments of chaos and decay, everywhere blue and white plastic bags floating aimless on dispirited puffs of air, then caught on the dry twigs and spines of the surrounding undergrowth, to flap back and forth like lost Tibetan prayer flags. And everywhere a pall, a stench of decaying matter and of slowly smoldering fires, heavy and acrid on the discouraged, drooping breeze, so far from the freshness of the sea.

He gazed at the world before him and suddenly remembered that this was the last year of the millennium. It was a depressing thought. He knew it meant nothing, of course, to the three goats, the implacably indifferent guardians of the realm to which he had come. But to him, it underscored another day without Nausicaa. He knew now he would not find her. Not today. Not tomorrow. The millennium was coming to an end. And then another millennium would begin. But he suspected that there, too, no Nausicaa would be awaiting him.

Jim had always admired Odysseus for his nobility in rejecting the almost miraculous vision of Nausicaa and a new life. He knew that Nausicaa was the greatest test of that great man of strategies. To survive Circe and retrieve his men from the pigs they had become was fine. To steer through the twin female horrors of Scylla and Charybdis was brutal, but well done. To listen to the Sirens and survive was clever and daring. To say no to Calypso with her offer of immortality and eternal sexual delight (after sampling it for seven years) was impressive. But turning down Nausicaa was his truest act of heroism. Nausicaa, after all, was Penelope, but twenty years younger. Nausicaa offered Odysseus the chance to cancel the Trojan War and his twenty-year absence from home by giving him a new start, with a new kingdom and a new bride. She offered what twentieth-century businessmen sought in their pliant secretaries, an escape from time, from aging, from the shadow of death. And Odysseus turned it down for Penelope and home. He turned it all down and chose instead to embrace reality. For Jim, it was that which made him a hero. Jim knew that he himself would not have resisted the temptation.

He turned the scooter around, gazed balefully at the three goats nibbling contentedly amid the trash and thistles, and then, with no great expectations, started on the long and winding road back to Engares and on to the Chora.

INTRAGALACTIC CHESS
ENCOUNTER

I

Microchips had been around for centuries, so no one was surprised when the Russian candidate, despite cutting-edge technology and deep cortical placement, was discovered with an almost perfectly hidden compendium of five hundred years of chess wisdom and was quietly but firmly placed on the first flight back to Moscow. That left Joseph as the undisputed representative of his beloved, blue-and-grey home planet, once, in the mythological, misty past, called Earth.

Joseph's ranking at the time was more than double that of the legendary American International (the archaic term used in those dark days) Grandmaster Bobby Fisher of the 20th century (old-style Christian calendar) at his height. The United States of America had, for obvious reasons, long ceased to exist, but Bobby Fisher's name had persevered through the centuries. And now, to his own astonishment, it was Joseph's turn to shine. Yes, it was he, he alone, who would shyly represent planet Terra at the Centennial Celebration of the

Intragalactic Chess Encounter (ICE). He felt a certain swelling in his breast, a kind of exhilaration that, to his consternation, felt clearly tinged with pride. He didn't approve of pride, but despite his best efforts, he knew it was part of him. That is who we are, he thought, with a certain melancholic resignation. He realized, though with reluctance, that he probably could not have become the world champion that he was, had he subdued entirely that dubious human characteristic. He sighed.

Worse than the inescapable problem of pride was the question of dear Milena. He felt torn at the thought of leaving her behind on good old Terra. Obviously, the chess tournament was serious business, it was a duty to humankind that he could not refuse, and at the same time it was unthinkable to imagine her accompanying him, as a mere tourist, on this lengthy journey to a wispy arm of the galaxy many light years away. It would not be easy to leave her behind, but it had to be done.

The authorities were impressed by Joseph's record-breaking global ranking and were eager to please this quiet, strangely modest man, about to embark on a heroic journey to represent planet Terra for the first time in history at the universally acclaimed Intragalactic Chess Encounter. But no one even broached the possibility of his fiancée accompanying him on his journey. Beside the prohibitive costs of sending a second person on a cryonic journey, everyone knew that the presence of a woman companion, not a fellow chess grandmaster, but rather a woman *per se*, whether designated girlfriend, partner, fiancée or wife, had been considered for centuries a harbinger of bad

14

luck. No one said those two words, of course. The very idea of luck had been disproven several centuries earlier. Yet, strangely enough, a shiver in the spine, a quiver in the stomach, suggested that even in intellectual circles, even in these enlightened times, the concept, though unvoiced and frowned upon, had not truly disappeared. Bad luck was like the legendary dragons that ancient mythologies had spoken of. Even long after they were disproven, they continued to lurk in remote caverns, curled around their evil, nursing their inner flames, brooding and awaiting a chance to once again exist. Joseph knew all this and could say nothing.

The World Body of Chess (the archaic word "Federation" had been discarded for political reasons centuries earlier) was proud of its champion. The entire world shared that pride. Even Milena was swept away, moved by the enormous stature that seemed to have descended, as if from the gods people once believed in, upon her gentle, kind Joseph. Yes, she shared the universal pride, but inside she was already feeling hollow. She understood that if he ever managed to return to Terra from his cryonic journey, whether victorious or not, she would be centuries dead and gone before his arrival. To lose him now, before their planned marriage could even occur, seemed a cruel twist of fate, but she knew there was nothing she could do. This was her sacrifice for the glory of Terra. She swallowed hard, put on a brave face, but felt a great ball of lead heavy in her stomach. Yes, she would have to remain on Terra and grow old, like everyone else, while Joseph, thanks to the standard cryogenic treatment, would remain thirty-three for the unfathomable number of Terran years it would take for him to reach his remote destination. Nothing could be done.

He, too, felt a ball of lead in his stomach when he thought of never seeing Milena again, but as the greatest chess player in terrestrial history, he had no choice but to bite the bullet and go forth to represent the human race. And so, much as he loved her, that is what he was about to do. One last time, the night before his departure, he gazed into her eyes, told her he would always love her, gently kissed her quivering lips, then turned around and didn't look back. He felt as if he were abandoning a gentle willow or a shimmering aspen tree. As for Milena, she never said a word. She knew the score.

II

Joseph entered the spacecraft the next day, accompanied by sober-faced technicians. He would be flying alone; all parameters would be handled from central command in the deserts of Western Australia. His lengthy cryonic sleep would be programmed to end at his carefully pre-determined arrival time. They placed him in a long tube, and an official, himself a bit of a club player, leaned over to whisper a final benediction, if one could call it that. "Good luck," breathed the nervous official, afraid of being overheard by one of the technicians. Even *good* luck was a concept discarded centuries ago. Joseph wondered if the friendly official's valedictory words were intended for the long journey to a remote portion of the galaxy or for Joseph's participation in the Intragalactic Chess Encounter that would follow. Before turning to go, the official, looking away, handed him a small square of dark chocolate.

"Eat it now, let it melt in your mouth. Something pleasant to remember, if any memories remain to you after your journey."

Joseph took the brightly wrapped chocolate square, popped it in his mouth, and gave the official a gentle smile of thanks. "Goodbye," he said. "Goodbye," said the official. And that was that.

When Joseph awoke, it felt as if no time had passed at all. The entire journey was a blank to him. He felt remarkably refreshed, as if his cryonic sleep had shaken the weight of time from his body, as if centuries floating free from the ego (and the superego, of course) had somehow cleansed him. Absurd as it was, he felt as if he had grown younger during the trip. To his surprise, the first thing that came to mind, before he even arose from his cryonic tube, was a verse from a poem his mother had read him as a child:

Since then—'tis centuries—and yet
feels shorter than the day
I first surmised the horses' heads
Were toward eternity.

He had never quite understood those resonant lines, nor had he ever seen a horse, but the verse felt right for that moment. He suddenly realized that he missed his mother.

Before he could be greeted by officials from the Intragalactic Chess Encounter, he was approached by a business-like technician who gently leaned over him and, without a word, inserted a small device into what Joseph knew must be the Broca area in the posterior inferior frontal gyrus. Joseph understood that from then on, all communications would come directly to his brain and be translated immediately into his own language. After being firmly lifted from his cryonic bed, he uttered or thought what he assumed to be the universally established customary salutation: peace. However, the two impassive officials, one on each side, returned a slightly elaborated version that he had never heard before: "peace and reason." That must have represented an advance established during the centuries of his frozen journey. He dutifully replied "peace and reason," and strode forward between the two of them, filled with vigor and eager to begin this important adventure, really the first great adventure of his life. Yes, he felt surprisingly fit. The only hint of time having passed since his departure from Terra was a slightly sour taste at the back of his mouth. It seemed strange to him, since the last thing he remembered from Terra, just before the journey began, had been a square of dark chocolate melting gently away in his mouth.

Joseph was offered a period of rest to recover from his long journey, though he felt as fresh as a daisy. He told the officials he was ready to join the tournament, but they insisted that he spend a designated period of time "decompressing," as they put it. He was given some transparent liquid with an unfamiliar tang to it. That it tasted strange was inevitable, he thought, so far from his home base back in the solar system. He was left alone in a quiet and shady room, where he slowly sipped at his drink through a transparent straw. The walls of his room were pale green, and a large window looked out on something that reminded him of the great Nullarbor Desert he had once crossed when in Australia for a Candidates Tournament a few years back (now, of course, a few centuries back, though he preferred not to think about it). Yes, he had chosen to take a bus across that uninhabited and dreary stretch of dried mud, just to experience almost three days of utter nothingness. He had already won the Tournament in Sydney and wouldn't play again until the actual World Championship match against, no doubt, the best player the Russians could produce. This journey to Western Australia had been an unplanned, spontaneous decision on his part. He had simply felt he owed it to nothingness to see what it was like. It was like nothing he had ever seen, nothing he had ever felt. It had made him uncomfortable. Yet he had been forced to see it once again, still finding it disconcerting, when he returned to the interplanetary launching site for this long journey. Strangely enough, however, here at the Intragalactic Chess Encounter, the view from his hermetically sealed window was not distressing at all. Perhaps he had changed since his visit to the Nullarbor.

III

Joseph slept profoundly, even though undisguised ceiling cameras made it clear that he, an alien from a relatively unknown corner of the galaxy, was being monitored or even studied. In the morning, an undramatic buzz awakened him. Feeling even fitter than the day before, he went to a small cafeteria area, where he was given another glass of the same bland, transparent liquid. It wasn't exciting, but it seemed to satisfy his bodily needs. An official led him to a lab where he took the obligatory physical and cognitive pre-tournament tests, before entering the almost sacrosanct (a word from the ancient past, he knew) precincts of the Intragalactic Chess Tournament. The authorities were polite but seemed uninterested in his possession of the all-time highest chess ranking in the recorded history of Terra. So, he took their tests, then waited, drumming his fingers gently on the tabletop. There was a period of silence. Then a lower-level official came forward, nodded to him, and suggested, via the universal translation device that he was growing used to, that he should follow him. The official led him down a long corridor lit by hard-to-discriminate indirect lighting. They came to a door with a simple, unpretentious label in black and white: Study Room 101. The official opened the door, politely gestured for Joseph to enter, then closed the door behind him.

There must have been some mistake, thought Joseph, as he gazed around the large study room with its austerely functional tables and chairs. The room was utterly silent and was filled with nothing but little androgenous-looking children, no older than five or six. They all were absorbed in their games, already underway, and no one looked up. However, one youngster was seated alone before a large green-and-white chessboard (how good that board made Joseph feel, as if, for a moment, he were actually back home). The child looked up at him expectantly. He walked diffidently over to the table and shook the child's small hand. They exchanged the customary salutation he had been taught the day before, and their personal translator implants conveyed the message. "Peace and reason."

As he took his seat, he saw that he was playing black and had already lost 25 minutes on the clock. Under normal circumstances such a time deficit would have been most disturbing, but when he considered his position as all-time champion of Terra's nearly two thousand year history of chess competition and the condition of the frail little creature, with its tiny hands, seated across the board from him, he felt sorry for the child and was happy enough to accept the time penalty for his late arrival, though, in truth, he could not see how his delay had been caused in any way by himself.

Looking at his diminutive opponent, Joseph prepared a variant of the French Defense. The child quickly fianchettoed both his bishops, swiftly advanced three central pawns, and seemed quietly content with how things stood. Joseph gazed at the board and suddenly felt swept with doubt. He made a timid pawn move, then finally cas-tled, but despite his apparent defense, he did not feel safe. After forty-five nervous minutes, the child with the tiny hands faltered, blunder-ing away his Queen. Or so it seemed to Joseph. Eight moves later, he found himself in mate. He was astonished. He congratulated his di-minutive conqueror on his fine Queen sacrifice. The child gave him a cursory smile but was already looking around for his next opponent.

By lunchtime, Joseph had lost two more matches. By dinnertime, he had lost another three. The following day, he lost another six matches, though one of them, he ruefully recollected, could have been converted, with a bit more courage, into a draw. By the end of the week, the tournament cycle in Study Room 101 was over. The little boy with tiny hands had come in third. Joseph, after thirty-six matches, had ½ point to his name. He was stunned. Those little children were geniuses, every last one of them. Truly, he had come to another world.

IV

At mealtimes, he had tended to drift towards a table of people seeming more his own age and they had accepted him. He had shaken hands all around (they seemed to be acquainted with the custom) and introduced himself. He accepted a platter of flat, almost weightless bread from his left-hand neighbor, then passed it on to his right. His Universal Translation Device assigned the word "mannah" to what they were eating, but the word meant nothing to him. The food had no taste, yet it seemed strangely filling. They were all drinking the same transparent liquid he had been offered upon his arrival. Even now, a week later, it still reminded him of nothing at all. Yet it, too, despite the absence of any flavor, left him feeling refreshed. And now that the tournament had drawn to a close, they were having a last meal, without fanfare, without medals or other honors, simply a last meal of post-tournament friendship, if one could call it that.

"How delighted I am to be here," said Joseph to the table at large. "How impressive the level of chess at this tournament, even amongst the five-year-olds," he continued. "No one back on Terra would believe it," and his voice trailed off as he remembered his home planet, now lost in the mists of countless light-years of space and time. "Yes," he went on, "I am honored to be seated here amongst you, especially as I have learned how advanced you all are compared to us Terrans." He hoped his words would not be considered a form of betrayal back home. But after all, it was nothing but the truth. And how would his words ever reach his fellows back home? He fell silent as he thought of the planet to which a return now seemed quite fanciful or even absurd. Everyone he knew would be long dead.

"I do have one regret, despite my joy at encountering this new world, this new universe," he went on. "You know, I haven't mentioned this before, but back home, I left behind my fiancée. Her name was Milena. By now, she will have been dead for several centuries, of course. But my heart aches when I think of Milena, for the truth is," he swallowed hard, then sighed in some embarrassment," the truth is, she was the love of ...."

"U.T.D. failure, BEEP, BEEP. System failure, translation malfunction, BEEP, BEEP, translation malfunction, BEEB, BEEP, U.T.D. failure" came buzzing through a veil of stillness from the devices implanted in all his fellows at the modest banquet. They gazed at him in some bewilderment. It was rare indeed for the universal translation device to fail.

Through the disconcerting buzz like that of angry hornets, he heard one simple sentence directed at him. "She was the *what?*" said the kind but puzzled young man beside him. "There seems to be a malfunction in my universal translation device."

Then Joseph understood what he had given up in leaving Terra behind. Love could now be nothing more than a memory. No one would ever understand what it was that brought tears to his eyes. He thought of Milena, her hair soft as the tassels on summer corn, her touch as gentle as a summer breeze, and he wished he had never become Terra's all-time world champion and come on what he now understood had been an irreversible intellectual journey to a realm far beyond the human. He realized, ruefully, that if he ever did return to Terra, the best he could hope for was to encounter some far-distant descendant of Milena, assuming she had done the sensible thing and, despite their pledge of eternal love, had married a fellow Terran and gotten on with her life. However, with Milena dead now for centuries, he felt it would be a betrayal to return and start anew, with someone hundreds of years younger, fresher, firmer, and utterly other. He was not sure he would even want to meet such a person. He was not sure there was any reason to return to Terra at all.

To make matters worse, light-speed communications after the results of the tournament were revealed showed a disappointing diminishment of interest in his mission back there on Terra. It was understandable. It hadn't occurred to the authorities back home that he would be defeated in every game he played. And by members of the under-six contingent, no less. It was clear to Joseph that, from having been a figure of heroic stature and hope, he must have become an embarrassment to humanity. Clearly, they would want to forget about him and his delicate mission. No, there was no point in returning. No point at all. He would remain where he was, surrounded by profound intelligence, silently nursing the dead weight of absence in his heart.

And so, with a sigh, he began to make his plans. He had seen neon-like posters with notices about chess training programs. Yes, he decided, since he had lost Milena forever, his best option was to stay here and enroll in such a program. With his habitual modesty, deepened by recent experiences here at the Intragalactic Chess Tournament, he imagined that after twenty years or so of diligent application, he might very well be admitted one day into Study Room 102 at the year's annual tournament, and be allowed to play, at last, against the twelve-year-olds.

That seemed a reasonable goal, considering the circumstances. And the officials, with what looked like a shadow of a smile, agreed to this humble alien's proposal. He would remain where he was as an open-ended guest, the only Terran specimen they had ever encountered. It might be interesting to see if he underwent any changes, any growth.

"Yes," they said, "he could stay indefinitely," and they gazed at him now with a strange emotion for which they had no word, but which made them wish they could somehow give comfort to this creature so very far from home.

LOVE

Du musst dein Leben ändern
Rilke

Dexter loved returning to grade papers late at night in Longfellow Hall. By then, his colleagues, of course, had all gone home to their pert wives, boisterous children, and silken golden retrievers. The building was deserted, and he felt a deep comfort in the stillness that pervaded the empty edifice like cotton wool. His lamp gave off a subdued yellow glow, and the large green desk pad blotter covered the surface of his small writing desk and spoke of peace and the gentle passing of time. As for the papers before him, they weren't bad at all. Snobbism aside, there were definite advantages to teaching in the Ivy League. Yes, some of the students were overbearing in their confidence, the unspoken knowledge that their fathers ran the country, perhaps even the world. But they were bright; they could still use the subjunctive, most of them knew the difference between "like" and "as," and some of them, despite their youth, had something to say. All in all, Dexter could not complain. He taught Greek tragedy, which he loved, and the students paid attention.

And here he was, late at night, alone in the empty building, contentedly reading their essays on Clytemnestra's morally ambiguous rage, on Cassandra's prescient helplessness. "Much like our own" flicked through his mind, but being young and healthy, he quickly dismissed the thought. He sipped at the remains of the hot chocolate he had made himself ten minutes earlier. Though lukewarm, it still tasted good. His wood-paneled office felt like a snug and elegant jewel box or perhaps the cabin of a first mate on one of those fine 19th-century clipper ships. Only instead of the crest of great waves beyond his window, there rose towering pines, spruce, and hemlock, shadowy sentinels guarding the stillness of the night. He had not lowered his blinds, but the darkness just beyond his window only added to the comfort he drew from the soft reading lamp, the dark wood stain of his paneled walls, the gentle embrace of his swivel chair, and the solid support of his writing desk.

But suddenly his concentration was broken. He had heard nothing, yet he was convinced that someone was standing now in the corridor just outside his office door. A chill ran down his spine. The hair on the nape of his neck stood up and prickled. Who could possibly be in the Language and Literature building at this ungodly hour? He sat in his chair motionless. Should he call out, should he make a joke, should he jump up and open his door and greet the late-night interloper? He sat there paralyzed. He didn't make a sound, he didn't budge. And suddenly he was certain, quite against all reason, all logic, all norms of science and society, that Jesus Christ was standing in the hallway, motionless, awaiting his response. Awaiting his invitation. He was convinced that all he had to do was call out and say "Yes, come in," and his whole life would be changed forever. The road less traveled by. He held his breath for what seemed an eternity. He said nothing. He did not call out. He felt like a rabbit trembling as a snake approached, flicking its tongue. And then the feeling passed, and he knew that the visitation was over, the presence just outside his closed door was gone, and he was alone, once again, in the deserted building. He took a deep breath, pulled out his grandfather's soft old handkerchief, and mechanically dabbed at the sweat pearling on his brow. He sipped the last of the now cold hot chocolate, piled the student papers neatly on his desk, took his windbreaker from its hanger, turned off the reading light, and left his office, closing the door softly behind him. Even so, he was startled by the sharp click of the lock snapping into place. He descended the stairs and, leaving the building behind, he walked briskly home, grateful for the company of the chill nighttime breeze.

**

It was a long drive, but sometimes on a weekend, Dexter would hop into his shiny new Beetle and drive to New York to visit his mother. She was a widow now, and he knew she was lonely. Having loathed his stepfather, Dexter had breathed a sigh of relief when he was gone. But he understood that his mother had loved him and found it hard to live without his burly, overbearing presence. They hardly ever discussed the man, the burden of his heavy presence on his son, and now the burden of his ponderous absence for his wife. His mother was, as always, happy to hear that he was coming. "And this time, Pumpkin," she said, "this time I hope you will help me bring clothing and food to Dorothy at the Catholic Worker. I can't do it using the subway, so you and your car will be really helpful, darling."

"Sure, Mom," he said. But he had managed to avoid such a visit in the past. This would be the first time, and he was uneasy about confronting a living Saint.

He arrived in Queens late on that crisp night in early November, and as usual, he and his mother sat up drinking tea in the kitchen. It always felt good, though he couldn't say why. He talked about Greek Tragedy, and his mother listened. Then she talked about the used clothing she had gathered together for the destitute winos on the Bowery, whom Dorothy looked after. She showed him a large basket of assorted fruit, with a red ribbon tied in a bow on top.

"Can you handle all of that, Pumpkin," she said, but he knew it wasn't really a question. "Of course, Mom, no problem." They hugged, and she went to her couch in the living room, while he went to the bedroom of his childhood, where he sank into a dreamless sleep.

The next morning, they had tea and English muffins. Then they went down to the car, Dexter laden with his mother's offerings. They piled everything in the back seat and off they went to visit her old friend, whom he had only met once, when they buried his childhood dog, Bambuk, on the Catholic Worker farm on Staten Island. He knew that progress had not been kind to Bambuk and that he no longer lay in quiet holy ground, but under one of the busy approaches to the Verrazano Bridge.

They took the Long Island Expressway into town, crossing over on the Williamsburg Bridge. Dexter tended to speed when traffic allowed, and his mother never said a word. For this, he was grateful. Soon enough, they found themselves approaching the Catholic

Worker on First Street. To his surprise, Dexter spotted a convenient parking space between trash bins. Clutching the bundle of clean old clothes, smelling freshly laundered, beneath his arm and swinging the gay basket of fruit from his hand, he waited beside his mother at the graffiti-stricken door. There was a pause, and he looked anxiously about, but the cold street seemed deserted beneath the pale winter light. Finally, they were buzzed in, just managing to squeeze through the entrance with the overly abundant basket containing its offering of the fruits of the earth.

There was a smell of Lysol in the corridor. There was a quiet group of men at a Formica table, huddled over mugs of steaming coffee. They did not look up. Then Dorothy appeared, tall, straight, blue-eyed, formidable. It was clear that she had been a beauty in her youth, and even now, aged and grey, she carried herself with the assurance of her younger days. She moved efficiently, with a grace that was not an embellishment, but an essential part of her mission. She had found herself in middle age, and there was no doubt or hesitancy in her movements, her gestures, her eyes. She knew where she was, here on the Bowery, here in this fallen world, and she knew why she was here. It had all become very simple for her. I am here to love my neighbor. And that was the business she pursued doggedly, insistently, quietly, firmly, and with finality. He could see what made her tick. It was God. Dexter was impressed but uneasy in her presence, as if she might be expecting something of him. So, after his mother indicated what they had brought, and she and Dorothy had exchanged the usual greetings and discussed a few matters, and all three had shared some sweet buns with cups of tea, he was eager enough to get back on the road. Dorothy thanked him for coming and looked, for a moment, piercingly into his eyes. Dexter had never, to his knowledge, been confronted by a saint before, and sheepishly, he looked away. His mother got up, she and Dorothy exchanged kisses and a squeeze of the hand, and mother and son were ready to return to the car and to the apartment in Queens.

On the drive back, he asked his mother how Dorothy could stand it: the hopeless men with their bulging red noses, their shifty eyes, their shambling ways. "Doesn't she get depressed, Mom?" he blurted out, almost in anger. "Those winos will never change. How can she stand it?"

He shifted to the passing lane and accelerated with some vigor.

"Pumpkin," said his mother, "you're right, she does get depressed. In fact, she gets depressed all the time. The last time I visited, she told me that she wakes up depressed every day."

"So how does she survive," Dexter replied, perhaps with too much of a worldly man's self-righteous indignation.

"She told me that she prays. At first, she feels nothing, as if she is praying into a void. But she keeps on praying, and the prayer finally calls forth a response, and then she feels God's presence once again. And that, Pumpkin, is how she is able to carry on."

Dexter, despite his instinctive distaste for the downtrodden—the irredeemably lost souls that had made the Bowery famous—remained silent. Dorothy's faith, in the midst of despair, humbled him. And for a moment, at least, he had a startling thought: a good person, a good human being, is possible after all, in this discouragingly banal and ordinary world of failure and endless disappointment. They drove the rest of the way in silence. His mother squeezed his arm, and no words were needed. But within himself, Dexter knew that despite sanctity, goodness, and hope, he himself would not be returning to the Catholic Worker.

***

The years had passed, and now his mother was failing. No one at the hospital/hospice spoke of her returning home. She was, after all, approaching 91, though her mind was still intact much of the time. But her body was giving out, a small bed sore had grown and grown so one couldn't bear to look at the raw cavity the size of a fist. He called every evening, sometimes finding her lively and alert, but at other times finding her silent, unresponsive, as if somewhere else. One of those evenings of distance, he concluded his one-way conversation with a sophisticated joke. There was a moment of silence, then a deep, guttural laughter of acknowledgment and pleasure. "Ha ha," she said. "Good night, Mom. Love you." Five hours later, still grading papers in his office as he had always done, the phone shrilled in the silence of the night. "Hello, is this Dexter?"

"Yes," said Dexter, "I'm Dexter."

"This is Dr. Babinsky calling. Sorry to trouble you in the middle of the night. Your mother has been a sick woman for many years now, as you know, and I have saved her many times. But tonight, I could not save her." Dexter dropped the phone and fell to the floor. He beat the linoleum with his fist. Then he groped for the phone and returned it to the receiver. The impossible had happened, as it must. Reality's most ordinary declaration, incontrovertible and utterly unacceptable. "Aujourd'hui, maman est morte." Impossible to translate, impossible to comprehend.

He drove to New York, he viewed the dead body, he arranged for the wake at the funeral home, he chose a casket, he drove with the entourage to the cemetery where she would join her husband, that man whom he loathed. Side by side, beneath the sod, together. He did it all efficiently, as it had to be done, all of it as in a trance. There were small speeches, there were the usual prayers. There were memories, one from a school fellow even older than she: "We were all in our classroom, and the teacher was just about to begin when suddenly there was the tinkling of a bicycle bell, and there she was, just outside the door, calling out, "Wait for me, wait for me. Here I am, here I am." The old man stood on the edge of the open grave, his eyes moist with the past. Others spoke, others remembered. He himself read from a poem by Theodor Storm that his mother had often recited: "Das aber kann ich nicht ertragen...." People embraced, people cried, and then they all went their separate ways, and he drove the long drive home and, late as it was, went straight to his office. Grading papers was more important than ever, and he dedicated himself to the task. This time, it was Oedipus Rex, and many of the students had decided to write about Jocasta, her knowledge, her blindness, and her torn inner self. He graded till all the papers were done and then he drove home to go to bed. He climbed the stairs, brushed his teeth in the bathroom, as on any other day, then, crossing the hall to his bedroom, took off his clothes, put on a comfortable grey pair of sweats, and crawled into bed.

As he was finally drifting off, but not yet there, caught somehow between being awake and asleep, between reality and dream, Dexter gazed up into the air above his rigid bed. And there, hovering just below the ceiling itself, was his mother, gazing down at him with an

abundant fullness of love. He could not move, he could only stare up-
wards. And there she was, stretching out her arms, reaching down to
pull him from his bed and into the embrace of her eternal love.
"Pumpkin," he thought he heard. "Pumpkin." Was it a dream? Certainly, he was paralyzed, as is so often the case in our nightmares. But
this was a strange nightmare, unlike any other he had ever had. This
was a nightmare of love. He strained, he struggled, he writhed and
finally forced himself to squirm away from his mother's loving grasp.
No, he was not ready to join her, even in the name of love. He shook
himself awake, he moaned a drawn-out "Noooooo," and his mother,
with a sorrowful smile, faded from the ceiling, from the room, and
from the world to which Dexter was still moored tight.

IF ONLY I COULD

For us, there is only the trying.
The rest is not our business.
T.S. Eliot

It started in the Village. It was Claudia's first time in New York, first time in America. Her friends had set her up with Joe, and it seemed to be working out. They danced all night, and she felt she could go on forever. As a teenager, she had wanted to be a ballerina, but her father had made difficulties. For men of his generation, a dancer was almost a prostitute. She loved to dance, but she couldn't oppose him, not in those days. Her one moment of glory, before dropping out, had been a rehearsal with Nureyev. He had come by to test the stage before his evening performance, and his partner hadn't arrived yet. So he took Claudia in his arms and they danced. She felt as if she had held her breath the entire time.

After the party ended, Joe offered to drive her to where she was staying. But just after passing Washington Square, he stopped on Waverly Place and said, "That's where I live. Would you like to spend the night here?" It was a quiet brownstone facing a chic Italian restaurant. She hesitated, then replied in her charming Italian accent: "It is possible you will not want to spend the night with me. I have something important to tell you." He waited. "I had cancer; I just had a breast removed three months ago." They sat in the stillness of the car. "Are you sure you want to go to bed with me?" Without a pause, Joseph said, "Yes." He couldn't have predicted what he would say, what he would feel. He was grateful, not just for her lovely presence, but for the suddenness of what had just occurred. He never felt sure what kind of guy he was, good, bad, something in between? At least, for this moment, he hadn't gone bad.

Not only was she lovely to look at, but she had a sense of humor. In his tiny artist's garret, there was barely enough room for his bed, his work desk, and his very large, long-haired Belgian shepherd. As they made love, Prince was both embarrassed and excited, and in the close quarters, his long bushy tail kept waving in the dark, brushing against both of them in a rhythmic, perhaps encouraging way. When they had finished, his wonderful guest said: "That is the first time I have made love to a man and a dog at the same time." Quite witty, especially with her charming accent.

He was not in love, but having said he would visit her in Rome, he did. His plane was two hours late, and yet there she was, beyond the glass, standing in a waiting area with no benches, standing as if she could have stood on her two firm legs like pillars forever. It was gazing down on her from the entrance ramp that he fell in love with that solid, stolid woman. When he made it through customs and was in her arms, he felt he was embracing both a princess and a peasant. He felt her long, slim fingers on his arms, their elegance and their strength, and leaning into her, he brushed against long, slender legs, well-formed and strong. This was not just a beauty, this was a woman with substance in the universe. Yet in bed, at first she was embarrassed, telling him ruefully that her remaining breast, look at it, had shrunk in sympathy with the missing one. He had passed his hand gently over the enormous scar, the empty space.

She took him on a touristic drive through Tuscany, to see the sights. Best was Pitigliano, that ochre town clustered on its ochre-orange cliff face, high against the sky. But later, as they were driving toward Porto Santo Stefano, a fishing town on the coast, Claudia suddenly slammed on the brakes. "What's wrong," Joe said. "Didn't you see that?" she replied, in an anxious voice. "See what?" he said. "That black cat that just crossed the road." "What about it?" said Joe. "I can't go on. I have to stop right here and not cross its path." "What?" said Joe, "Are we going to stay here forever?" "No, "she said, "you'll see, someone else will come along and take up the bad luck." And indeed, a minute or two later, another car did come by, and then Claudia was willing to travel on. But as things turned out, despite her hopes, the other car did not pick up her bad luck, after all.

The following summer, Joseph was returning to visit Claudia in Rome after a month-long artist's residency in Segovia. When he saw that the train was passing close to Lourdes, he sheepishly got off. He wandered about the garishly touristic town, walked the peaceful Via Crucis, and spent the night at a cheap hotel. In one of the tourist shops he bought a plastic bottle of holy water to bring to Claudia in Rome. One could never be too safe. When he arrived, she greeted him as before. How happy he felt to be in her strong slim arms. He gave her the souvenir bottle from Lourdes. She took it and said thank you, but he never knew whether she drank it later on, sprinkled it on her scar or her remaining breast, or simply threw it out. She had told him that one of her brothers had died of liver cancer and another in a plane crash. Her parents had already lost two children, she said. She felt responsible for whatever remained of their happiness. Though she made the sign of the cross like everyone else, he wasn't sure how far her faith went. He envied those who believed, but he also pitied them. And watching them in church or on a pilgrimage, he hoped there was a God worthy of their faith. In any case, if your train is passing by Lourdes, you have to get off and give it a try. What else can you do if you are in love?

Claudia lived in a penthouse above Campo de'Fiori. The grave statue of Giordano Bruno, burnt alive in that square in 1600, frowned grimly upon passers-by below. In the daytime, the square was a bustle of shoppers and vendors, with a great variety of cheeses, fresh vegetables, cuts of meat, and a few wine shops lining the storefronts. The sound of a fountain's trickle could be heard all night long. There were cupolas in all directions, and swallows would dart through the sky in the evening, catching invisible insects with their rapid acrobatics. And all night one could hear the chimes, at first on every quarter hour, later just on the hour itself. Each church had its own sound, but one bell seemed to provide a basso continuo, a deep tolling that lay behind all the other chimes.

When Joe, his feelings deepening instead of diminishing that second summer, proposed that Claudia help him find a long-term residency or perhaps a position teaching studio art at one of the local academies, their relationship began to change. The more the romance blossomed for him, the more he wanted to move to Rome and live with her permanently, the more uneasy she seemed to feel. And he remembered that it had all begun so romantically for her, in New York, in a strange place, with a strange man, dancing all night in a world that was not her own. It had been an affair, just what she wanted, what she needed. And now it was he, in a strange world, surrounded by a mellifluous language he only partially understood, who was more and more charmed by her, her apartment, the Campo de' Fiori, the nearby Piazza Navona, the bridge over the Tiber leading to Trastevere, even the flow of the very names themselves; it was all utterly charming. In New York, it was she who was charmed, it was she who fell in love. In Rome, it was he who swam in romance, who fell deeper and deeper into a kind of trance. But for her, Rome was reality, her reality, not just her circle of women friends, her ex-husband whom she avoided, the shopkeepers, all of whom she knew by name, but the very hospital there on an island in the drab Tiber where her left breast had been removed less than two years before. Rome, for her, was not a place of romance. Joseph, she saw, felt carried away. She could not be carried away. And when he began to insist on seeking a position, finding connections in the art world, she grew more and more uncomfortable. She didn't want a husband, not even a romantic husband. She had already had a husband, and she knew what that was like. She had wanted a lover, a romantic lover, a dream lover, what she had had briefly in New York. But this was drifting toward reality, and she could not see a happy ending.

She did not help Joseph make connections in the art world, and he returned to New York at the end of the summer. It was there, around New Year, that he got a phone call from a total stranger. The Italian spoke good English. He said he was Claudia's cousin and was calling with some serious news. She had been on vacation in Paris, had left her hotel to wander the streets, but could not find her way back. Bewildered and lost, she was finally taken to a hospital. They had done MRIs, CT scans, and the usual diagnostics. It was bad news: her breast cancer had metastasized and gone to her brain. She would probably die within a year.

Joseph returned to Rome for a last visit. She welcomed him in her apartment, but as a friend, no longer as a lover. Another lover, darker and surer, had staked his claim, and there was nothing to be done, nothing to be said. Joseph stayed on for a week, her American friend, the dance partner from Greenwich Village, the eager stranger in Rome. One night, they stood in the living room looking out at the Roman night. Against the sky, one could make out the dark, rounded shapes of the cupolas all around. And even that late, there were swallows still darting through the night sky. As always, church bells chimed, and behind the chimes was a deeper bell, tolling in the distance. Joseph could hear the trickle of water from the fountain below, he could see the sober statue of courageous Giordano Bruno in the square below. He gazed out and, without thinking, from his blind American heart, he exclaimed: "What a wonderful place to live, Claudia."

They had never discussed the return of her illness. It was simply understood, a shadow for which no words could be commensurate. But now she acknowledged it for the first time and the last: "If only I could."

He took her elegant, aristocratic peasant hand, and she allowed him to. But it lay limp in his grasp, as if it had nothing left to do in this world. There was nothing to say. He gazed down at her hand and finally let it go. Then in silence, he returned to his room. The next morning, she accompanied him to her door. "Addio," she said, and that was all. "Addio."

Three months later, news came to New York. She was dead. Her circle of friends generously put his name in the newspaper notice of condolences, along with theirs. He was grateful to have been included in their loss. And he remembered the holy water from Lourdes that he had brought to her in a plastic bottle the year before. He would never know if she had used it or thrown it out in despair. All he knew was the outcome and that, passing through Lourdes, he had gotten off the train to buy a cheap bottle of holy water. Hope against hope. Grasping at straws. Lord I believe. Help Thou my unbelief. Well, he had tried. What else could he have done? Miracles are rare indeed. But what else can we hope for?

JOY

Who can understand the human heart?

Everyone envied them their good fortune and their happiness. Carol was beautiful and young, free of vanity and pretensions. Her eyes were bright green and always ready to smile. She loved to paint, and that is what she did. There was a stillness to her canvases that gave each scene, each depiction, the flavor of eternity. A grey cow, sitting placid beneath a grey palm tree, appeared prepared to remain motionless till the Second Coming. The huddled houses of the fishing village at night, with just a streetlamp casting a weak glow, seemed to reveal their quiet communality on her canvas. The painting was a study in shades of black, with a slightly different hue for the night sky, the quiet lagoon, the rising forested hills, and the dark blocks of the houses themselves. In her most celebrated painting, the downtown warehouse of the provincial capital with its empty pier stood in naked symmetry in the midst of a deep silence. The government center had bought that canvas and placed it in a prominent position in the entrance hall. On all her canvases, time stood still, and the local upper crust, from both state government and the regional branch of the federal university, was fascinated and bought everything the local gallery displayed.

James was a professor of American Literature, presenting, as best he could, the special flavor of his home country to Brazilian students, both eager and laid-back. Because he hated the Puritan in himself, he loved teaching *The Scarlet Letter*. Most of the students could not accept Hester's final self-immolation, her deliberate return to the town of her torment, her insistence on placing the hated symbol of her sin upon her breast once again, even when the townsfolk had finally abandoned their self-righteous cruelty. Adultery, their church had made clear, was a deadly sin, but in their own hearts it made their blood throb and their eyes glisten. He himself was torn by mixed emotions. He was filled with awe and admiration, contemplating Hester Prynne's passion and pride, but he was also terrified. He assumed that Hawthorne had felt the same way.

Back home, in their bungalow on the edge of the lagoon, James engaged in perhaps the only manual labor of his life: he built the frames for Carol's paintings and he stretched the canvases. To his surprise, he was able to do it all: measure the boards, saw them clean, create triangular wedges to support the corners, nail them together, place a supporting cross brace down the middle of the larger frames, measure and cut the sturdy canvas, use clumsy pliers to pull the material over the stretcher bars, then finish the job with a stapler, tightening the canvas to its frame. He was not good with his hands, and he had never built anything in his life except childhood sandcastles at the beach, so he enjoyed the unaccustomed sense of fulfillment that came when he leaned each finished, clean canvas up against the wall. He had the pride of a seneschal, a valet of art. His father had been a skilled draftsman, and his sketches of the very young and very old were filled with an ironic, yet warm, perceptiveness. James had inherited neither his father's warmth nor his talent. Ironic perceptiveness perhaps.

And so they lived on the edge of the lagoon, envied by all. She painted, he prepared her canvases and, of course, his classes. At night, they would eat fresh shrimp from the fisherman living in the neat wooden shack next door. Quite often, in late afternoon, they had the chance to watch Valdir perform his artistry. Standing in the shallows on the edge of the lagoon, he would rock his whole body, then uncoil, throwing the shrimp net in a whirling circle with the grace of a ballet dancer, the eternal elegance of a Michelangelo. Right arm still extended, feet firmly planted in the muddy bottom, he would watch his net sail in its perfection, then settle gently on the water and slowly sink out of sight. Bringing the catch in reminded James of Marcel Marceau, that beautiful mime, the quiet harmony as the slender old fisherman slowly, very slowly, hand over hand, drew in the collapsing net, rich with its delicate load. James felt surrounded by art. Carol and Valdir were both possessed, without knowing it. But what about him? Did he have an art?

Despite his doubts, stepping back from himself, from the two of them, he could, on occasion, see how fortunate they were. Their days were sunny and warm, their nights cool and pleasant. The village was tranquil, nestled between forested hills with troops of small monkeys and the distant roar of Atlantic surf. How could one not be happy? Yet, now and then, despite the screens, a high-pitched whine close to his ear would remind him that even in paradise there are mosquitoes.

***

When summer break at the university was approaching, they managed to book passage on a Spanish cruise ship heading for Antarctica. On the ship, they ate well, tried their hand at bridge with Argentines much more skillful than they, and played ping pong on a table that rose and fell with the rolling of the waves. They laughed at their ungainly situation and James grinned, remembering Charlie Chaplin's brilliant shipboard dining scene in *The Immigrants*. How he would have enjoyed the ping pong match, with the swaying deck, the tilting table, and only the small white ball keeping its proper place in the air. Dizzy from the ship's motion and the illusiveness of the ping pong ball, they abandoned the table and, clutching each other's arms, descended the narrow stairwell to their cabin in the lower depths. He managed not to vomit, despite his nausea, but for James, making love that night was out of the question.

The jumping-off port for the Palmer Peninsula was Ushuaia, the southernmost city in the world. The water in the harbor was greener than Carol's eyes, James thought, but icy cold and crystal clear. It suggested something eternal, beautiful, and boundless. In fact, it had nothing to do with Carol's warm eyes, and he felt foolish for having thought so.

Having the balance of the day to explore, they took an ancient taxi inland, towards the snow-capped mountains rising beyond the town. They shared the ride with two other tourists from the ship, an elderly couple, wiry and fit. Loren and Sue had lived for decades in South America but had now retreated to Washington, D.C. He was on assignment for National Geographic, doing a photo article on Argentina, its beauty, and its troubles. When the unexpected tour to

Antarctica was announced, they couldn't resist. Luckily, there was an Argentine research station on the Palmer Peninsula, so it was easy to convince his employer to include the tour on his bill.

Arriving at the base of the mountains, they gathered fallen branches from the woods and dragged them towards the middle of a wide hollow just beneath the ramparts of friable red stone. There they built a small bonfire and huddled around, warming their hands. The snow-capped mountains rose above them. Loren was a true outdoorsman and, when a couple of mountain climbers arrived in a second battered taxi, he decided to accompany them up the steep face. After half an hour, they disappeared from sight, enveloped in a sudden snow cloud. James wished he had gone with them, though he realized he had neither the skill nor the gear for such a venture. The others all had sturdy mountain boots, and he, absurdly, was wearing tennis sneakers. Excluded from the real adventure, he waited with Carol and Susan down in the valley. They were talking away happily, so he busied himself returning to the nearby stretch of forest to gather more wood for their blaze. He piled some of it on and the flames leapt up, the dry branches crackled, and Carol and Susan, still chatting away, laughed in their bulky orange Antarctic Touring gear.

It wasn't long before the three figures reappeared high on a col, returning from above the snowline. When they were all gathered round the fire, watching the charred logs shift and drop, the mountaineers talked about mountains, while bars of chocolate went around. One of the strangers revealed that he had just gone on a mission a week before to retrieve the frozen body of an American climber lost on Aconcagua. It had been a difficult rescue, if one could call it that, since the dead American was about six foot four and frozen solid. He said that in a month he would be leaving for an expedition to Mount Everest. Listening to them talk, James wondered where he fit in. He had always dreamed of Mt. Everest, but he suspected he would never get there, not even to base camp. Having a dream was easy. Incarnating it was something else.

As he listened, he watched Loren, who had squeezed down between Carol and his wife. Loren smiled at Carol, then murmured something to his wife while handing her an elegant bar of Toblerone chocolate. Though listening to the mountaineers, James kept his eyes on the elderly couple. He could see that they were comfortable and secure with each other. He could see that, old enough to be his parents, they were still in love. He envied them and wondered: "Could he ever achieve such a thing, could such a thing ever happen to him?"

**

The passage through the roaring forties lasted most of the night and into the next day. It was as rough as had been predicted, and James and Carol took turns vomiting. But then, on the far side, the ship came out into the clarity of a low-lying midsummer sun, and, in the distance, a bank of white clouds signaled the ice-clad coast of Antarctica. The late afternoon never really ended, and the half-light, James felt, was both enchanting and disturbing, as if they were on another planet. Suddenly, a few hundred yards away, a blunt-headed sperm whale surged almost perpendicular from the water, rising ponderously, like a slow-motion lift-off at Cape Canaveral. Then it fell back with a crash and disappeared. There was utter stillness, as if the coldly beautiful world was holding its breath. Then a second massive creature burst from the sea, the same trajectory, the same slow ascent, the same falling back, as it, too, disappeared beneath the icy water. All eyes were turned to where the whales had risen and then vanished. At first, there was an awed silence. Then someone called out, "Welcome to Antarctica," and the spell was broken.

Yes, they had made it to the edge of Antarctica, but James was dissatisfied. Cautious due to the threat of drifting ice, the captain was loath to put into the narrow harbor, the destination listed on their itinerary, the spot where Scott had overwintered. He didn't want to be stuck with eight hundred tourists on the ageing Cabo San Roque, surrounded by ice floes, with diminishing food, diminishing toilet paper, and increasing anxiety. So he anchored just beyond the natural harbor and James had to content himself with glimpses of the tops of the masts of the two research vessels that had made it inside. How he envied them.

As for him, for Carol, and the others, they could gaze at towering glaciers and bluish ice floes. They could watch the ominous dorsal fins of killer whales and the frantic leaping of penguins from the water, followed by their stolid waddle inland. But they themselves were only allowed to visit two islands off the Palmer Peninsula. The great adventure at last, thought James, but they were not permitted to set foot on the Antarctic continent itself. It was little consolation for him to remember that even the legendary Christopher Columbus had never set foot on the American continent. Nor had Magellan, in fact, completed his famous circuit of the world. He had died from a poisoned arrow in the Philippines. And before them all, there was Moses, perhaps the most unfortunate, not allowed by Jehovah to enter the

Promised Land. At the thought of these predecessors, he gave a wry smile. But he was not reconciled.

Carol, on the other hand, loved the ice cliffs, loved seeing the killer whales, loved the Adelie penguins hobbling on the ice, loved the endlessly lingering twilight of the polar summer. She sketched everything she saw, even her fellow tourists. As far as she was concerned, they were indeed in Antarctica. And she was happy. Her happiness irritated James, though he knew it should not.

On one of the islands where they were able to land, James carried camera equipment for Loren. They walked down a long stony beach towards the snorting, belching, roaring agitation of Southern Elephant Seals in their breeding season. Fully twenty feet long, enormous males challenged each other for dominance. Loren photographed them in their vicious, slow motion combat, neck braced against neck, bulging chest against chest, yawning jaws twisting forward to tear out flesh, then twisting away. Except for their bleeding wounds, they looked like Sumo wrestlers. Indeed, the heavier combatant normally was granted his space, and the smaller male, overwhelmed by close to four tons of aggression, would back off in defeat, then turn to the water for comfort. James was impressed by these battles and was glad to be helping the photographer with his varied cameras, lenses, tripods, and other paraphernalia. Though he loved to travel, he had never carried a camera. He wasn't sure why. This was as close as he had gotten. Carol took a batch of snapshots with her Kodak. They would develop them back in Brazil. But James knew they wouldn't be like the ones that Loren was taking for the National Geographic.

When the cruise ship steamed north, James and Carol parted from their group, including the couple from National Geographic, during a brief stop in the Falkland Islands. Wandering the roads around Port Stanley, they experienced three or four seasons in just a few hours. There was brilliant sunshine, then violent gusts of wind, then a snow flurry, then a hazy calm, then sunshine again. They walked along the coast, they walked amongst the pastures. They had afternoon tea with a couple of red-cheeked Welsh sheep farmers, who invited them in. The farmers said it was a hard life, but a good one. As for Argentina, it was a foreign country to them. No one in the Falklands even spoke Spanish. The friendly couple ended up offering them a room for the night and they accepted. It was genuine hospitality, but James understood that to be proper guests in that small house, they had to sleep silently. So, in the sagging bed, he gave Carol a peck on the cheek, murmured good night, and rolled into himself.

The next morning, they were given a warm send-off (almost no one ever visited the Falklands, after all) and boarded a small plane for Rio Gallegos, the nearest town in Argentina. They had read about Cabo Virgenes and its huge penguin colony. Even after their Antarctic adventure, Carol wanted to see more. Back in southern Brazil, she had painted the sad little penguins that arrived on their beach during mid-winter storms, exhausted and dying. Only one that they knew of had survived, living alone as a sentinel in the garden of the governor's palace. She had been jubilant to see living, thriving penguins finally, and she was eager for more. James, still feeling thwarted by their failure to set foot on the continent itself, feeling cheated out of the culmination of the great adventure, thought that perhaps a visit to the remote tip of South America, with its vast Magellanic penguin colony, might provide something to fill the void.

In Rio Gallegos, they hired an eager young taxi driver for the day. Carlos knew nothing about penguins, had never even heard there was a colony, but was willing to give it a try. With the rather vague destination of Cabo Virgenes, they headed south. There were, of course, no road signs. At first, they passed through fenced-in sheep country, and all they saw were great pastures of grass and endless flocks of dirty beige sheep. After an hour or so, the fences disappeared, and they began to see the soiled woolly coats of dead sheep lying beside the road. They were a bit shocked, but Carlos considered it normal, since there were endless sheep and no fences, and he just kept driving along, looking as if he doubted the gringos knew what they were doing. After another half hour there was a change: instead of dead sheep, they began to find dead penguins beside the dirt track. Carlos perked up, never having seen a penguin before. In fact, as he explained, this was the furthest he had ever driven from downtown Rio Gallegos. Carol looked sad, gazing at the helpless small bodies, but James, still smarting from the Antarctica anticlimax, took it as a good sign. Soon they would arrive at the colony.

And then they did. The road, by now, was more sand than dirt, and the taxi was laboring along in second gear. But at the next modest rise, they suddenly saw the South Atlantic shimmering beneath them. It was filled with penguins. Thousands and thousands of them dotted the water, and as the surge mounted and waves crested, many of the penguins simply surfed ashore. The waves were huge, the penguins very small, but they were utterly at home in the surge. Carol stood in the wind on the edge of a dune, gazing out in triumph. James himself felt inspirited, as if perhaps his Antarctic funk might be lifting. He glanced at Carlos and could see that even the taxi driver was happy to have come along, and not just for the forty dollars. The stiff breeze blowing in from the ocean, however, was cold. Carlos, wearing just a windbreaker, finally retreated to his taxi. James and Carol, after gazing their fill, dropped back from the edge of the cliff, taking shelter in a sandy bowl surrounded by clumps of scraggly dune grass. It was there that Carol saw a tiny penguin hidden in a hollow it had carved from the sand beneath a thick cluster of grasses. James watched as she bent closer, almost cooing. She reached forward, still murmuring, and held out her hand. Suddenly she pulled it back with a jerk. Still hunched over the penguin's nest, she exclaimed, "He bit me. He bit me!"

She was not aggrieved; she was filled with wonder, transfixed with joy. Her eyes sparkled with the miracle of life. This other being had touched her, had made contact. "He bit me," she murmured again, standing up next to James. He took her hand, and without realizing it, gently began to caress her cold fingers. They were trembling. Then he stooped and kissed her on the lips. It was a long, soft kiss, and he felt as if a dam had suddenly broken inside him. "Could this be what had been missing? Could life really be like this?" he thought. And for a moment, at least, he truly loved her.

CALYPSO

For Michael, who called it a story

He called her Calypso because he was bewitched. She was a modern dancer. Every move she made tingled in his nerves, leapt across his synapses. When she shifted weight from one hip to the other, while drawing out a cigarette and placing it between her lips, he felt like melted wax. He stood and stared. He had no volition. If she gave him a glance and a nod, he followed.

On those late summer weekends, they would scour the backroads for honkey-tonks. A string of year-round Christmas lights, a smoke-filled embrace of darkness, cheap beer, easy music, shadowy bodies letting go on a Friday night. As Calypso danced, every particle of her body, of her being, was in consonance, resonating to the music, at home in the beat. Even the Texas Two-Step became a sensual intrigue as it passed through her body. And he would follow, drawn along by her spell. She was so good that strangers in cowboy hats would come up to their table between dances, put a callused hand on Jim's shoulder and, with conspiratorial warmth, intone: "Say, now, young fella, you're a professional dancer, ain'tchu?" That's how good she was. She smiled whenever it happened. She knew who the pro was. And so did he.

In bed, Jim felt like Odysseus returned to Ithaka, home at last. He ignored the obvious contradiction, that Ithaka was his hero's real home, with patient Penelope, his long-suffering wife, and domesticity about to reclaim him. For Jim, the cradle of Calypso's hips felt like destiny, and entering her was like arriving where all lines meet, that impossible realm beyond which lay nothing. He understood that had he been Odysseus, he would never have left Calypso's magic, unreal island. For him it would have replaced the Ithaka of mere daily life. Intellectually, he admired his hero for his sturdy resolve, his final insistence on returning to reality, but knew that he himself would never have renounced the illusory gift of the shimmering immortal. In any case, dismissing the obvious contradictions from his mind, he would sink with utter bliss into an unbearably remote and exquisite arrival, though the bed in which they lay stood firmly in unremarkable Ohio. Such was their life together.

Then his wife returned. She had, in fact, been planning to leave him for some time and had gone off on an exploratory trip, during which, high in the beauty of the Sierra Nevada, with its remaining patches of late summer snow in the highest north-facing granite clefts, she had found her next love. Now she was back to arrange affairs, set up a new house, and install her new man. It was a bit awkward, but not unexpected. They both knew their passion was spent and would not return. It was just one of those embarrassing transitional moments one has to go through. They did their best to behave properly. Jim never mentioned Calypso. She never mentioned her new man.

One evening, they attended a piano recital by a local talent. They had seats in the front row, below the pianist, who, with eyes shut tight, was swaying, mesmerized, through the painful enchantment of a Chopin Nocturne. Everyone loved it. Jim had tears in his eyes, and the audience applauded at length. Then it was intermission. Suddenly, a tiny princess appeared before them. It was Isadora, the dancer's seven-year-old daughter. She stared at Jim and ignored his wife. Standing with the unperturbed erectness of the very young, she said: "I know who you are. You are the man who left his toothbrush at our apartment." And having delivered her message, she disappeared into the crowd. Jim's wife gave him an amused look but accepted his silence. Their house was big enough to accommodate the two of them and the silence that lay heavy between them. A month later she was gone.

And life with Calypso continued, like an impassioned dream. One weekend, they made it all the way to the Cumberland Gap, left their car at a grassy parking lot, and hiked up and over a misty mountain range. Hitching back to their car at the end of the day, they got a ride with a charming blond in a convertible. They spoke of their long autumnal hike and how they were trying to get back to their car at the trailhead. They praised the beauty of the mountains, the softness of the haze. They praised the beauty of local Blue Grass and asked her to play some on the radio. She gave them a frightened look and said: "I'm sorry, but we don't listen to music none. It ain't right. Except, of course, we sing in church. We praise the Lord. That's the Lord's music. That kinda music is OK." She gave them a timid smile and a gaze, of sunshine and dew, from china-blue eyes. She was beautiful; and to Jim she seemed sad, like a yearling alone in a wide, empty field. Touched, they said nothing more about Blue Grass or Country Western. Somehow Jim felt tainted, worldly, and almost ashamed. But that evening they found a remote honky-tonk and danced till closing time. There in the bar, they didn't feel guilty. They just felt alive. They just felt joy.

And then, a few months later, Calypso was offered another job, with a dance troupe three states away. She had to go. She had no choice. Jim had to stay, but he looked forward to visits, despite the distance. What's 450 miles to a man in love? And so she packed her car, she and Isadora gave him a kiss goodbye, their hound dog licked his face, and they were gone.

The weekend they had chosen for his first visit was not auspicious. A snowstorm swept down on the Midwest, but Jim figured he could push his way through. After two hours, he found the Interstate closed down by ice. He called Calypso to explain his delay and went to a local dance club in a nearby town to wait it out. It was a gay joint and the supple dancers looked at home. Bereft of Calypso, Jim found himself embarrassed, unsure, perhaps even fraudulent, a feeling he sometimes had had in the past, before meeting her, when he would wander casually into a remote Black juke joint in the back country, where all the homefolk danced better than he did. Calypso could usually pull him out of his sense of inferiority, sweeping him into her aura of animal harmony, body and beat, sound and soul. But this time, Calypso was not with him, and the few women on the dance floor were clearly there for the superior grace of their gay friends. Jim asked a few to dance, he did his best, but he was kidding no one. He kept calling the highway patrol, and at 3 A.M. the Interstate had been cleared for traffic and he was off.

He reached Calypso's new place at blue-gray dawn. No one answered the bell. He walked around, found the kitchen door out back, turned the knob, and entered. He walked through the kitchen into a dining room, and suddenly she appeared, soundless, gliding like a ghost, accompanied by her hound Argos, whose nails clicked on the cold linoleum floor. She took his arm and said: "I'm sorry, I didn't think you'd make it through. My bed is occupied." Argos sniffed at his trouser leg and wagged his tail. Jim's stomach felt filled with lead. An elfin creature, a delicate faun, drifted silently from the bedroom towards the front door. Calypso guided her new love forward and, with a gentle pat on the very bottom of his buttocks, ushered him out the door. But it was over. The love of his life, Calypso, had moved on.

He staggered out to his car and got in. He drove back to the Interstate, its ice now melted, and eight hours later was safely back home. He parked in the carport, stumbled to the back, fumbled with his keys, dropped them, picked them up, entered the house, kicked off his shoes, threw off his winter coat, took a leak, mechanically brushed his teeth, then fell into bed. He awoke sixteen hours later to a chill dawn, made some coffee, and readied himself to start his new life.

But it wasn't that simple. He was haunted. He feared he might be going insane. He had no one to talk to, and, desperate, he called a stranger's number in the Big Apple. It was Calypso's former husband. He felt like an idiot, an idiot in despair.

"Hello, is this Jake? My name is Jim. You probably don't know who I am. Forgive me. I'm a guy out in Ohio and I fell in love with your wife. Your ex-wife, I mean. Forgive me, but I'm going out of my mind.

I just can't stand it. I'm crazy about her and she's left me. I think I'm losing my mind, you know what I mean?"

After a brief silence, a deep voice came from the other end of the line. "Yes, I know what you mean. The same thing happened to me, didn't it?"

Jim thought he even heard a chuckle. He swallowed and then went on, rambling, stumbling, repeating himself, begging forgiveness, talking of love, despair, anguish, entangled in a web of helplessness, making an utter fool of himself, he was sure. Jake just listened. Then finally he interrupted:

"It sounds to me as if you think you can justify your life through love."

"Of course, I do, what else is there?" There was a pause on the line.

"It can't be done, my man. Sorry. You can't justify your life through love."

Jim said nothing as he tried to take it in. Then he apologized again for the absurdity of the call.

"Don't worry about it," said Jake. "Let's just call it a *Mitzvah*. Goodbye, good luck. You'll recover. I did." And there was a gentle but definite click on the other end of the wire. And life, indeed, went on.

Forty years later, Jim was traveling, buying art in Ecuador. The best stuff was in Cuenca, but he decided to take a little break and visit a nearby mountain town with a tiny zoo and lots of horses. He ended up spending three or four days in Vilcabamba, walking along the river, feeding bedraggled animals at the much-neglected zoo, strolling around the town square, and playing chess with the locals. He also went on a day-long ride high into the hills to visit a waterfall. He was old, but he could still ride. At a steep ridge, the path narrowed, and his horse suddenly shied. He kept his saddle, and the guide was impressed. Jim was just relieved and felt lucky. The dip in the waterfall, when they finally got there, felt like a baptism. Jim had to lean on the guide as they descended from the grassy field where they left the horses to make their way down the steep drop to the side of the mountain stream. He was glad they had come. He knew he would never be able to do that simple hike again.

Wandering around the formal town square on the last day of his visit, he noticed a sign he hadn't seen before. Modern Dance it declared in bold letters. He climbed the rickety stairs to the second floor. There sat a woman in her sixties with a well-sculpted face, a black leotard, her body still perfect. He said hello and discovered she was an American, settled years ago in Vilcabamba. She had been a modern dancer in New York back in her youth. Almost idly, Jim asked if she had known his Calypso, back in the day. He used her real name, of course. The woman's face lit up.

"Did I know her? We were friends for over twenty years. Where do you know her from?"

Jim told his story with the efficiency that forty years of perspective afforded him. He mentioned the new lover Calypso had found out there deep in the Midwest, the man who had displaced him in her heart, her bed.

"Oh," she exclaimed, "that must have been Carlo. She brought him along when she came back to New York. They lived together for years. They were a happy couple. It finally fell apart, as things do, but it was good while it lasted. They were together for at least ten years. How funny that you should have known them."

They chatted some more, then Jim took his leave. The stairs creaked as he made his way down. So, too, did his knees. He passed slowly through the small garden in the center of the square. He bought a chocolate ice cream cone and licked it round, as he strolled back to his room. How strange to meet a friend of Calypso's here in the remote mountains of southern Ecuador. But how much stranger to discover that he was feeling an unexpected tranquility, a kind of mellow warmth, a kind of happiness, in fact. The news, so unexpected, about Calypso came as a thunderbolt, but a gentle one, if such a thing could be imagined. He was astonished, surprised, and yes, even happy, to hear that the faun-like creature who had displaced him had not just been a one-night stand, that in fact Calypso had fallen in love with the man who slipped into her bed while he, Jim, had been waiting out an ice storm. Indeed, St. Teresa was on to something when she said: "God writes straight with crooked lines."

As he entered the gate to his hotel, Jim breathed in the early evening air and felt a quiet contentment. Though his joints ached, there was no ball of lead in his stomach. He knew that he was irretrievably imbedded in old age, in a realm beyond the searing ecstasy and pain of passion, but it was not a bad place to be. The companionship of ambiguous memories was neither hollow nor empty. Filled with a diffuse sense of well-being, he looked back at the darkening mountains behind him and felt a soft flood of gratitude for the lingering twilight around and within.

HOW SAD THE FLESH

La chair est triste, hélas ! et j'ai lu tous les livres.
Mallarmé

He had at least four thousand books. They lined all the rooms of his rambling house.

Poetry was in the living room, from floor to ceiling, beside the stone fireplace. Ammons to William Carlos Williams. On the opposite wall, in perfect order, American 20th-century fiction, from Agee to Nathaniel West. One wall of the comfortable den downstairs, dominated by the trusty old wood stove, was filled with literary magazines, the other with European literature arranged by language: French, Italian, Spanish, Russian, German, with a few Scandinavian works sharing the shelf. Everywhere he looked, he saw the comfortable embrace of all those books he would never read again. He felt surrounded by quiet old friends with whom there was an unspoken understanding. Nothing needed to be said. They shared the same world. Their presence confirmed his very existence. Whether he touched them or not, he was content.

He had not read all the books, of course, but the ones that remained unread, alas, were proving quite disappointing. He had worked his way methodically along the two shelves of miscellaneous contemporary writings, but except for the rather blustering optimism of the good-hearted Alexander McCall Smith and the wry, ironic goodness of Haven Kimmel, he found little that resonated in the chambers of his soul. He was beginning to despair. He felt it would be redundant to return to the company of Tolstoy, Dostoevsky, Chekhov, Hawthorne, and Melville. And Camus was already part of his bloodstream and needed no revisiting. *Aujourd'hui maman est morte.* In fact, she had been dead for twenty years. Walking slowly from room to room, he would pass beside his orderly rows of books, silent sentinels always in attendance, solemnly regarding the palpable weight of absence. There was one empty shelf reserved for photos of his dead, and from there, his mother gazed at him with eternally unanswered questions. And would continue to do so. As long as he was there.

Despite what seemed a comfortable stasis, at times a glimmer of hope would stir feebly within. Perhaps, despite his age, there was still time to leave the house and give the world, or himself in the world, one last chance. Yes, he decided to his own surprise one gloomy midwinter day, he would gird his loins and, leaning heavily on his mahogany cane, leave his retreat one last time.

Turning to his academic past, he soon was able to conjure forth an invitation to teach a one-month seminar in modern American women poets at a remote branch of the Federal University in Brazil. He had established that country's first graduate program in American Literature nearly half a century earlier, and several of his students, now elderly chairs or even program directors, remembered him as part of their exuberant youth and were happy to honor him and themselves by inviting him back. And so, in early March, retired Professor Sterling packed summer clothes in one suitcase, and Edna St. Vincent Millay, Sylvia Plath, Anne Sexton, Mary Oliver and his personal favorite, Sheryl St. Germain, in a smaller traveling bag, locked his front door, and left his keys with a neighbor, who, in the solidarity of the old, drove him to the local airport an hour away. As they shook hands at curbside, Prof. Sterling wondered if they would ever see each other again.

His reception in Teresina was warmly chaotic. After much backslapping at the small airport, he was escorted through the humid night air to an air-conditioned car, which brought him and his two welcomers to a small but elegant hotel where he would be staying for the duration. After drinks in the deserted bar, he was led to the elevator, into which all three squeezed, along with his suitcase and traveling bag. They left him in his room, with further slaps on the back and a chorus of "Seja bem-vindo, Prof. James." In Brazil, you were always addressed by your first name as a kind of universal seal of goodwill and total acceptance. He entered the room, brushed his teeth, arranged his few books on a narrow shelf above his bed, and then collapsed. Ten hours later, he awoke from dreamless sleep, surprisingly refreshed.

His course went well and his students divided into two camps: those who adored Mary Oliver and those who adored Sylvia Plath. It seemed that they were becoming, respectively, acolytes of those sibyls of life and of death. As for Prof. Sterling, he was delighted to be back in the classroom after five years of retirement and felt rejuvenated by the poets and by the eager students bubbling with youth. He was glad he had come.

One evening a colleague and fellow bachelor invited him out for a beer. They went to a bar-restaurant, its patio filled with the usual youthful Brazilian exuberance: the clinking of glasses, a samba sounding in the distance, and a sea of voices, unrestrained, in the flush of life. They chatted about the depressing political realities of the day in both their countries. They chatted about urban versus rural, north temperate versus tropical. Then a local singer, accompanied by a guitarist, took the small stage, and they stopped talking and prepared to listen. James was already a fan of the raw and plaintiff music of the Brazilian hinterlands, the *sertão*. Sipping on his beer, he leaned forward in anticipation.

Gazing out at the crowd, the singer, a slender woman with ash-tinted chestnut air, smiled, lifted the mike close to her lips, and, like a soft caress, whispered the simple words "Boa noite, gente." The background noise subsided, she looked at her accompanist, and they began. Her voice was deep and made James think of molasses. So, too did her gentle swaying. He was mesmerized.

She sang with a throaty sensuality, and to him it all felt very tropical, humid, and romantic. She concluded her set with "Asa Branca," a long-time folkloric favorite throughout the country.

Her looks reminded him of the great writer and beauty Clarice Lispector and somehow an unexpected surge of energy from the distant past raced through him and, to his shock, after her set had ended and she had taken a seat at a nearby table, he found himself walking toward her and asking in his most polite Portuguese if by any chance she was related to that great visionary writer. The woman looked up at him, bewildered and flattered. She demurred, but said she wished she were related to her. "You look so much like her," the old professor said. From the adjacent table, his abandoned drinking partner looked on with amusement and approval. And so it had begun.

Of course, they had nothing in common, but James was utterly happy. No doubt she was flattered that a serious gringo professor was interested in her, but she must also have been calculating what this relationship might bring her. He couldn't blame her. Singing in local bars was fun, no doubt, but hardly could have provided her with any-thing substantial. James was happy to wine and dine her and she seemed happy enough to join him in his hotel room almost every night. Like a number of other aspiring Brazilian women, he quickly noticed that she always wore a broad-brimmed hat in the sun and plenty of sunblock at the beach, thus retaining soft, smooth, very white skin. For James, this late-life encounter with the simple joy of gentle, pliant flesh, was overwhelming. Although she turned her back as she drifted into sleep after love, he was filled with gratitude.

James found looking at her a pure pleasure and she enjoyed be-ing looked at. One morning, after descending for the usual magnifi-cent breakfast at his hotel, James asked Lena what she thought of Clarice Lispector who was, indeed, her country's most revered and in-novative fiction writer and proto-feminist. Lena, like everyone else, admired Lispector, but then confessed that she had never read her. James hid his astonishment and, their lengthy breakfast complete, he led her to the nearest bookstore and bought her Lispector's *The Hour of the Star*. She seemed to be touched and asked him to sign a dedica-tion to her, as if he himself were the author. With great care, he in-scribed some mellifluous words, declaring his admiration and esteem. As she took the book from his hands, like a precious offering, her long, soft fingers touched his own, and it felt to him like some kind of benediction.

But as the weeks passed (his teaching stint was coming to an end), and the harmoniously uneven relationship continued, two things became clear. She could not, she told him, bring herself to read the book, though she had set it in a place of honor on a shelf just above her bed at home, where she still lived with her aging parents. She even showed him the shelf one day, when he came by to pay his respects to her fine-boned elderly mother and stone-faced father. There was Lispector, just beside her breviary, a fashionable self-help book on affirmative thought, and two collections of Bible stories retold for the modern reader. With a slight reluctance, but no embarrassment, Lena declared that, although she had attended college for almost two years, she had never developed the habit of reading. In fact, she had never read an entire book in her life. When James expressed his wonder, she was neither mortified nor angered. She just laughed her throaty laugh and said yes, it was strange, but that's how it was. When James asked her to bring the book along to the park where they often walked in the shade of stately trees, she complied. They found a wooden bench under a magnolia tree, and there James read to her, as if to a child. She sat and listened, delighted. When he finally stopped, she told him that she loved listening to his voice and that she found his accent in Portuguese most charming. "Please read to me again someday," she pleaded. He said that would be a pleasure and, arm in arm, they sauntered from the park and continued on the graded path that accompanied the turbid tropical river making its sluggish way through the middle of the sleepy city center.

James had traveled a good deal and Lena had never left her hometown. She seemed to know nothing of the outside world but listened with interest to his stories. James told her about Portugal, suggesting she would enjoy a visit there, since it was a country that spoke the same language. She looked dubious but listened like a well-bred child. He told her that he had been on a beach in southern Portugal when the Americans landed on the moon and everyone had gathered round to congratulate him, as if he himself were an astronaut.

"The moon?" she said. "The moon? Americans were on the moon?" And then she went on: "And the moon in Portugal, is it the same as our moon here?" And then she moved on to more earthly matters: "And Portugal," she said, "is Portugal the same size as Brazil?" All he could do was put his arm around her slender, naked shoulders and give her a long and gentle kiss.

It was the year of the World Cup and the two of them enjoyed watching the matches on the big screen in the shopping mall. By now, Prof. Sterling's duties at the Federal University had ended, and he had plenty of time to accompany the soccer matches transfixing the rest of the country. They were dismayed, along with everyone else, at how badly Brazil played, and the stunning seven-to-one defeat by Germany cast a pall over everyone gathered in the Mall's vast food center with its enormous screen. They continued to watch throughout the week and were not surprised when Germany won the entire competition. As the post-game celebration was in full swing, the announcer, carried away by excitement, shouted above the roaring crowd: "It is utter pandemonium here in central Berlin, here in Alexandre Platz, the streets are surging with people shouting and cheering, joyful chaos here at midnight." Disconcerted, Lena looked down at her wristwatch, looked into the eyes of her adoring gringo lover, and softly, in a bewildered voice, said one word: "Midnight?" He reached over, pulled her close, and gave her a tender kiss. There was no other possible response.

Once in a while, as the weeks passed, they discussed sex. Lena confided to him that she had told her priest of her situation. She didn't want to be a sinner. The priest had said that as long as she genuinely tried to convince her lover to marry her, she was not sinning in the eyes of the church. She felt relieved by his words, but at the same time felt a responsibility toward the holy sacrament of marriage. And so, as novelty faded into a comfortable part of daily routine, every once in a while, she would bestir herself and go on strike, come to his room in the hotel and lie on top of the bedspread, comfortably watching her favorite soap operas, but refusing to slip between the sheets or remove her thin dress. James, to his surprise, instead of anger or frustration, found himself touched, moved by her simplicity, her innocence, her guileless stance, placidly gazing at the TV, gently obeying her priest and fending off his wandering hand, oblivious to the indifferent universe, stretching endlessly beyond the familiar night sky, sure of her priest, her church, her guardian angel, and her ultimate destination there in the heavenly choir. The soap opera, the Virgin Mary, and the Holy Spirit were more real to her than any time zone, or the dimensions of any European country, or the report of an alleged landing on the moon. She was in good hands.

As the weeks passed, James noticed how the details of daily life took up much of Lena's attention and her psychic space. Arranging doctors' appointments for her aging parents, driving them to those appointments, going to the pharmacy to get the various prescriptions that they needed, seeing her own specialists, her dentist, her hair-dresser, her manicurist, kept her on the run. And then there were those endless phone calls with her girlfriends, married, divorced, with ungrateful children or, like she herself, with none, listening to their problems, their sorrows, their regrets. And attending evening Mass on TV with her aged mother, already blind and inexorably grow-ing deaf, as well. Yes, her life was quite full, though she never strayed beyond her hometown, and the well-known intricacies of its avenues, traffic circles, peripheral highways, connecting bridges, one-way streets, inconvenient red lights, etc. But she was happy enough to squeeze Jaime, as she called him, into the niches that appeared in cor-ners of her busy days. And he was content to read all day, to write, to take a solitary stroll, as he awaited the dinner date, the evening to-gether, the occasional touch of her unblemished soft skin, her immac-ulate flesh.

Whether they made love or whether she was on strike, just gaz-ing at her gave him a kind of misty contentment, and he would plac-idly stroke her arm, immersed in a sense of well-being.

But then, after almost three months of the pleasures of compan-ionship and of the flesh, of periods of sensual bliss alternating with wryly ironic intervals of blessed, virtuous deprivation, of pleasant strolling in the shade beside the muddy river slowly flowing toward the sea, of several excursions to the bookstore in the mall where he bought more books to stand unread but revered on her dedicated shelf, a crisis suddenly loomed. His visa was about to run out. He would have to leave. He would have to go home.

And so, with tears in his eyes, James said goodbye. At the airport, she gave him a kiss overflowing with feelings that she had, to a certain extent, devoted herself to denying. Even she understood that the visa trumped her hoped-for sanctification of their union. Now that he was leaving, she felt able to make room for genuine tenderness. James, himself, had felt almost nothing but tenderness the whole time. They said good-bye, he walked towards the departure gate, he looked back at that lovely creature with her slender frame and ash-blond hair, her dark eyebrows giving her away, and suspected he would never see her again. How sweet, he thought, how sweet the flesh, that tangle of ambiguities, prohibitions, and ironies. How sweet the flesh had been in this final iteration, in its pockets of possibility, its moments of unencumbered, temporary bliss. He wondered, despite the depletions of old age, the dreary complexities of official documentation, the vast expanse between her world and his, whether he might not manage a return, after all, sometime, somehow.

Good-bye, Lena. How sweet the flesh and how very sad. He boarded the plane and leaned back into his seat, feeling suddenly tired and old. And as he awaited lift-off, what came to mind was the poignant final word on everything: The Lord giveth and the Lord taketh away. Blessed be the name of the Lord. But a stale taste hung heavy on his tongue.

TILL IT'S GONE

It was decades before he ran into her again. By then, he was bald and twenty pounds overweight. He was dining alone in the town's most chic restaurant. He rarely went there because, though the modern frescos were attractive and the food good, the meals were over-priced, and he had remained as stingy as in his youth. But tonight, planning to hear the local band in the bar next door later that evening, he had decided to splurge for a change. Emerging from the men's room (these days every meal at a restaurant involved such a detour), he bumped into a slender woman, narrow-shouldered, perfect in her high heels, just leaving the ladies' room. Mumbling excuses, there in the narrow vestibule, they saw whom they had bumped into. Clare was unchanged, utterly unchanged. Embarrassed, touched, without a thought, he said: "I have nothing but good memories of you, that's all I have, nothing but the good." "Me, too, Joey," she had managed to whisper, with a brief look of affection, before hurrying back to the somber husband staring at her from their table.

Joseph never saw her again till the day before she died. Her daughter had come to town to be with her mother in her final suffering. The husband apparently hovered round the hospital bed much of the time, unwilling for anyone, including God, to share in his prize. He told friends who called that she wanted to see no one, because he wanted her to see no one. He had even tried to prevent her only daughter from coming, but to no avail. Her friends, however, were afraid of him and didn't show up. That's the way he wanted it. She was his wife, his love, his love alone. He had loved her back in high school, but only in his sixties, after marriages, divorces and deaths in both their lives, had he finally captured her. And now she was slipping away, and he was furious. He paced all day, but in the evening, he went home to drink, and Clare's daughter, from her mother's bedside, called the boyfriend from thirty years before to say: "If you want to see Mom while she's still here, you better come right away. He's gone home, he's drinking, he won't be back tonight." And so Joseph went to say goodbye.

Her fingers were puffy with edema. So, too, her face. But the eyes were the same, even as she lay there dying. Eyes sparkling with mischief, ready to find a laugh in anything. Joseph moved a chair beside her bed and sat down.

"Hello, Clare," he said.

"Joey," she answered. He took her swollen hand and softly caressed her fingers.

"I am so glad to see you, so glad," he managed to say. She smiled from her cocoon of prednisone and soporifics. The daughter gave him a nod and quietly slipped from the room. They were alone. But what could he say? What can one ever say, up against the wall?

"Remember that time when Shep ate that big steak right off the dining room table?"

"It was a roast, a whole roast. I went to the kitchen to get the vegetables, and when I came back, there was nothing on the table, and he was licking his chops."

They laughed and laughed. Life had been good. Now it was leaving. What could one possibly say?

"I was a bad guy, Clare. I'm sorry."

"Don't be silly, Joey, you were just a kid. A forty-year-old kid, that's all."

They held hands and said nothing. Time passed. He gave her a sip of water and she sighed. She mustered a wan smile, but her attention drifted, as if to another presence in the room. Her grey eyes looked both spunky and preoccupied. After a bit, her eyes closed. She seemed to be drifting off. He kissed the puffy hand he had been holding since sitting down beside her. She didn't open her eyes, but she smiled and gave him a slight squeeze.

"So good to see you one more time," he whispered, as he arose. She squeezed his hand again but said nothing. He looked at her puffy face and couldn't bear it. Without a sound, he left the room.

***

Fresh to town, he had been lucky to meet her. She was leaving a Christmas party, and someone in the crowd had called out, "Looking good, Clare." Drawn by that remark, he had turned around in time to catch sight of a slender, pert creature in elegant high heels, slipping into a camel hair coat. She had looked so good that without another thought, he had grabbed his own Duffel coat and bid a hasty farewell to all.

He caught up before she reached her car. They shook hands, exchanged names, and discovered they both loved to dance. They agreed to meet at a cocktail bar where the best local singer was performing the next night. And that is how it began. Even before their rendezvous at the Round Table, he knew how lucky he was.

She danced with controlled abandon. She had a flare, pizazz, energy to burn, but everything wound tight, like an Arabian mare, sleek, reined in, but ready to go. They danced every number, rock, foxtrot, cha-cha, and even a waltz. She made it all look easy. They were bathed in sweat and never stopped till the band took a break. She told him, then, that she was a supervisor at the nursing home and that she had six kids, but he couldn't believe it. She was slim and smooth, with a mischievous grin, *joie de vivre* incarnate. Though she was French-Canadian, she had lost the language of her ancestors, but not their bounce, their verve. She was a ball of fire, and he was very happy.

After a while, he began to drop by her house. He met the six kids, a terror of teenage boys, all rambunctious, all disdainful of school. None of them even brought their schoolbooks home with them. Only the lone sister seemed to enjoy her studies, seemed to feel a richness coming from the lectures, the classroom, the books themselves. As for the boys, once escaped from their obligatory classes, they reveled in basketball, baseball, and, when the lake froze solid, ice hockey. The T.V. was on twenty-four hours a day. The only books in the house were anthologies of *Readers Digest.* Joseph was an English prof. at the regional junior college, no great shakes, but books were part of his life. They wouldn't be in this household, he thought with regret. Yet she was so utterly charming, a bundle of energy and goodwill. How could she raise six kids, and dance all night long, and get to the hospital by eight A.M. every day? But she did. She did it all, and never thought to complain.

He knew he was blessed. But he was also discontent. Charming as she was in manner, lovely as she was to look at, when he tried to discuss things beyond the scope of daily occurrences, events, nothing happened. It wasn't just books he couldn't discuss with her. He couldn't even manage to share his lifelong preoccupation with mortality. Coming from a Shakespeare class, one day, he tried to engage her in a discussion of *les dernières choses*. He had been teaching the very problematic, almost tragic comedy, *Measure for Measure*. A lovely virgin is desired by a cruel judge, who will execute her brother unless she gives her "sweet body" to him. She is, of course, bewildered and appalled. She visits her beloved brother in prison and tells him he must die. Unless. "Unless what?" the desperate young man responds. She explains the Judge's heinous offer of his life for her "sweet body," but is assured her brother is too noble to entertain such a thought. To her shock, he groans and replies: "Oh Isabel, Death is a terrible thing."

"What do you think of that?" Joseph said to his slender, eternally young love, as she smoothed a goose in rosemary, thyme, and butter. "Death," she said. "Funny you should mention that. I was talking to an old timer in the nursing home just yesterday. I said to him: 'So, how you feeling today, Benjamin?' And he says, 'Well, Miss Rabideau, not too good, not too good.' So I say to him, 'Why, what's the matter, Benjamin?' So he says, "I think I'm just running out of steam, Miss Rabideau.' So I say, 'Benjamin, how old are you, anyway?' So he says: 'Well, Miss Rabideau, I'm 104, going on 105, if I get to July.' So I say: 'Well, Benjamin, that might explain why you're feeling a bit tuckered out. Not too many people get to 104, now, do they?' So he says to me:

'Well I'll be a monkey's uncle. You know, Miss Rabideau, you're right, I guess I just didn't think of that.' Now what do *you* think of *that*, honey?" And that was their discussion about mortality.

But then he remembered her effortless grace on the winter ice, a twirling, swirling of pink jacket and blue jeans in the frozen cove, dark pines behind her, grey sky above. And his own clumsy strides, his bent ankles, his inability to stop. And her smooth transformation to concertgoer up in Montreal, those sophisticated high-heeled slippers she insisted on, even in winter snow and springtime slush. Her camel hair half-length winter coat, its snug embrace. Her delight in the concerts, though he wondered if she had ever gone before. Yet seated in the loge, she looked a perfect fit. As if that was where she belonged.

She never said a word, but after a couple of years, Joseph could feel that she was waiting for something. Though they never discussed money, it was clear that her salary was barely enough to keep the household afloat. She was happy with her lover, but he understood that she needed a husband. However, when he thought of the TV on day and night, the shelves of *Readers Digest,* the wild kids full of life, but oblivious to everything he believed in, and the impossibility of discussing the mysteries of life and death, he felt himself balk. He felt he would have to marry not just his delightful, slender dance partner and elegant concert date, but her six children as well. Indeed, that was reality, and it was too much for him. They never discussed it, but when New Year's was approaching, she gently, but firmly, informed him that, alas, she had a date. He was miserable, but he understood that he had brought it upon himself. He had lost her. The man she went dancing with on New Year's Eve had plenty of money, did the right thing, and four months later, they were married. He could blame no one but himself.

And now she was dying. As he walked home through the silent streets, he wondered if he hadn't made a dreadful mistake thirty years before. He had enjoyed her sparkling eyes, her cheer, her humor, her lovely body, her ebullient spirit, her roasts, red potatoes, and Brussel sprouts. Why hadn't he married her? And what about love? Had he loved her back then? He remembered that at the time, happy as he was, he thought he was not "in love." And now, wandering home in the dark, he was returning to an empty house, its walls lined with silent books. It had been decades now since his home had been blessed by the unfathomable love of that same dog Shep, who, against all civility, but in consonance with his wolfish nature, had gobbled down Clare's entire roast so long ago. The empty house, a shell, awaited him.

How foolish he had been thirty years ago. Now, old and bent, he was able to feel a tenderness that the armor of his ego had not permitted when he was young. As he trudged homeward, it dawned on him, in the dark winter stillness, that against the grain of his self-centered instincts, his quietly ruthless egoism, he had actually loved her back then. In fact, he had loved her all along. But only now could he admit that to himself, knowing that tomorrow or the day after, she would be gone forever from the face of the earth. The old hit song suddenly slipped like a dagger into his belly: "You don't know what you've got till it's gone."

There was slush on the ground, and his feet were growing cold. He would have to make himself a pot of steaming tea when he got home. He hoped there was a bit of honey left in the cupboard.

LAST LOVE

She was the last love of his life. When she flew home to Bulgaria, he wandered around in a daze. For three months, he never fell asleep before dawn. He was from a previous generation and hardly understood how his cell phone worked. But Maria, adept with all electronic equipment, Maria who looked at him with pity and scorn when he didn't light up at the name *Pearl Jam*, would send him text messages, and he learned to open them. A typical message would say: "I dreamt of you this afternoon. We were making love, very slowly." It killed him.

He took a leave of absence and concocted a scholar's visit to Sofia. Through the academic grapevine, he managed to arrange guest lectures in three departments at St. Kliment Ohridski, the oldest University in Bulgaria. Its most famous alumna was Julia Kristeva. He came fully prepared. For American Studies, he presented an in-depth analysis focusing on irony in Frost's "The Road Not Taken" and "Design." For the Dept. of English, he spoke about Conrad's belief in simple virtues in a world without meaning. He talked about work and rivets. For Feminist Studies, he analyzed some short stories by the great Brazilian proto-feminist Clarice Lispector, focusing on a painful study of a woman in old age, "In Search of Dignity." The students were shockingly competent. The buildings of the university were all falling to pieces, the walls were chipped, the faded paint peeling. The desks had broken loose from their moorings and were misaligned. The students, however, were not only bright and eager but seemed to speak whatever language was needed with a striking familiarity and ease. George was astonished to hear youngsters sounding like genuine *cariocas* from Rio, though they had never left Bulgaria in their lives.

The lectures had been a ruse, an excuse for the trip, but in fact they were deeply rewarding. And George felt embarrassed at the genuine interest of the students, the obvious commitment they had to their work. In this impoverished country, the young knew how precious their studies were. Back home, most students couldn't be bothered to read their assignments. Back home most students were in college to drink, party, and fumble their way through sex. They complained about the price of their books and how they didn't have the money to pay for them. But they always had money for beer downtown. Here no one had money for anything; most texts were run off for the students on the departmental copy machine, but everyone knew the value of thought, the value of study, the value of literature. He was ashamed of being an American.

He had met her at a summer writing retreat. She was lean and angular, and she glided like a wolf. Her grey eyes could not be distracted. They were icy cold, precise, unerring, and they cut straight to the core. They had seen it all and could not be deceived. She was thirty years younger than he, but she knew everything. The rush that filled his breast was predictable and embarrassingly trite. But that she would return his passion had never occurred to him. As they sat in his roomy old Mercedes at the edge of a golf course at twilight, watching the elk emerge from the woods, he expressed his astonishment at her feelings: "I'm an old guy, I'm bald, I'm getting a paunch, how could you possibly fall in love with me?" She gave him a scornful look and simply said: "You don't know anything about women." To that, he had no reply. They watched the elk. One of them had a noble set of antlers so large one almost pitied him his magnificent burden.

After a long silence, he asked her what they would do about it. She replied with the confidence of a general laying out battle plans beyond dispute. "What will we do? No problem. We will sleep together for the next three weeks. Then you will go back to New York, I will go back to Sofia, and we will never see each other again." Yes, she simply took his breath away.

"I can't do that," he said. "Either this is forever, or it's nothing at all." There was a brief silence.

"O.K. I'll send my husband an email, asking for a divorce." She really took his breath away.

And now he was in Sofia, lecturing at the university and waiting to follow her lead. And soon enough, she led him out of town to a ski resort, where he could ski all day, and she could work on finishing her present project. She sat in bed, propped up on the pillows, her laptop balanced on her legs. At night, she was gentle and softly breathed into his ear: "Slow, my love, slow, slow." It was almost unbearable. So good it was sad.

But her husband was an intelligent man and did not scream or flail about or beat her. He stayed home and took care of the kids, seeing through his wife's pretexts (showing a visiting scholar around the country), but saying nothing. He called to report on the kids and to ask about a cough medicine for the eldest. He asked how the visiting scholar was enjoying the countryside. He put their five-year-old daughter on the phone. "Hi, Mama," she chirped, "when you coming home?" And he waited for it to pass.

She finished her project and suggested they go to a lovely small town of cobbled streets and old churches. They spent a day in Koprivshtitsa. A sunny day, but pleasantly cool. They attended a church service. George felt cleansed by the flowing waters of the foreign tongue, the foreign chants. But when Maria told him that she had spent her honeymoon in this quiet retreat, George felt uneasy. When she mentioned that it was her husband who had suggested she take him to visit this ancient village, he felt even more uneasy, as if they were being observed, being followed. He was impressed by her quiet husband's sagacity and felt that without any demonstration, he was reaffirming his position in her life. George was filled with his love, of course, but he was beginning to feel like an interloper.

Necessity drew him back to New York. But while suffering, as if from an amputation, he found a publisher interested in bringing out a collection of short stories by an up-and-coming younger Bulgarian writer. He sent an email to Maria and suggested they translate the book together. She said yes. He suggested they work on neutral ground, let us say in Budapest. She said yes again, but her letters now seemed precise and practical. They almost seemed to shiver in their starkness, shorn of former endearments, like sheep on the cold slopes of early spring.

He got to Budapest first and rented a small apartment close to the river. He had a few days to kill before her arrival, so he played chess in the park and went to jazz recitals at night. The jazz was good, the chess players were excellent. But it was all just a prelude.

He could hardly fall asleep the night before her early morning arrival. Groggy, he went to the terminal to meet her, but her bus had come in ahead of schedule, and she was gone. She had his address and was probably heading for his apartment. He hurried home, but before he got there, he saw her tall, angular form stolidly trudging down the street, shouldering the North Face backpack he had bought her in Banff. He called out and rushed up to her. He threw out his arms and squeezed her in an impassioned embrace. She broke free, and in a fury whirled around to face him.

"Don't touch me," she hissed. "Don't you dare touch me!"

He stood there in shock. "What happened?" he said. Everything felt unreal.

"What happened," she exclaimed. "What happened? What happened is I fell out of love. I never thought that could happen, I thought love was forever, but it isn't. I just fell out of love, that's all. Don't you dare touch me!"

He carried her backpack the last block, and they entered the small elevator leading to his apartment. He was stunned, and they said nothing as they rode up.

Once in the apartment, she went to the bathroom to freshen up after the all-night bus ride from Sofia. She came out, drying her face with a hand towel, but she didn't smile. George felt an enormous weight pulling him down.

"How is this possible? I thought it was love. I thought it was forever," he staggered forward with useless words.

"I thought so too. I thought it was love. I thought it was forever. But I was wrong. Don't you dare touch me!"

"But why, why did you come to Budapest?" he fumbled on, as noise from the morning traffic began to rise from the street.

"I wanted to see. I didn't know what I would feel. I can't explain it." He moved toward her, and as if waving a stiletto, she hissed, "Don't touch me!"

There was nothing more to say. She did not get on the next bus to Sofia, and George didn't throw her out. They worked on the book for three weeks and, despite the sense of suspended animation, of the iciness of empty space filtering into the apartment to encase them, the project advanced satisfactorily. It was as if the work of translation could free them from the death of what had been. At least that is how George felt. The work saved him from total despair. Or at least it delayed the drowning. The translation progressed, they took occasional strolls through the city streets and along the river, and on these strolls, crossing the street, Maria would take his arm as if they were an old married couple. It was bewildering. It was unbearable.

At night, it was even worse. They would enter the large double bed, each from their own side, for there was no other sleeping arrangement possible in the small apartment. And she would stretch out, straight as a corpse, and lie there beside him, never reaching out, never shifting close enough to allow even a random touch of his body, nothing. All he could feel was the warmth emanating from the proximity of a body now inhabited by an alien being, a body he still yearned for with anguish and knew he could never touch again. And she would begin to talk in a soft, bedroom voice, almost whispering, speaking of her beloved grandmother, of the agony of her mother's deathbed, of her anxious love for her two children, talking with a quiet intimacy, as if to an old and familiar husband, long beyond the realm of passion. Once or twice, he tried to touch her, but she would leap up, screaming, "Don't touch me!" then quickly subside and quietly return to a comfortable monologue of familial reminiscences. And for three weeks, those were their nights together in Budapest. It was, to George, incomprehensible, a tantalizing nightmare, a weave of warmth and distance, intimacy and utter estrangement, and he could not imagine any sequel, any escape. He lived in a suspended animation of hopelessness, like an insect wrapped in the soft elasticity of a spider web, and only the daily task of translation provided a suggestion that normal reality still existed, that life, indeed, still went on, that death was just a shadow lying somewhere beyond.

And then the book was done. Maria packed her things, George pulled together a final dinner. Maria said she didn't care whether her name appeared on the cover of the book. George accompanied her to the terminal, where she entered the night bus to Sofia. He stood outside her window, looking up at her. She looked as if she were already gone. In fact, he understood that she had been gone even before she arrived. He should have known from the diminished flow of her emails, from the absence of tender words, that the trip to Budapest was coming too late. He had lost her months ago, though how or why he would never know. Just as one doesn't know why one falls in love, one cannot really know why one falls out of love. Every miracle has its countersign. Every miracle leads to loss. He doubted that dignity could compensate.

He stood there mute below her window. Finally, as the driver entered and turned on the engine, Maria leaned out and said, "Don't feel so bad, George, it would have ended sometime anyway. This is for the best. Don't worry, you'll forget me. You'll be OK." And then there was a shifting into gear, a slow movement forward, and the great old bus rolled out of the terminal, bearing Maria back to her real life. George just stood there until the bus was lost from sight.

That was twenty years ago. George hasn't forgotten a thing. Yes, life went on. There were books, travels, even minor affairs. He supposed one could say that he was OK. But he knew that in Budapest something had been extinguished that mattered more than anything else in his life and that nothing could be done about it. Not then. Not now. Not ever. And always, it seemed, there lingered about him the faint, but persistent smell of a candle snuffed out.

CENTERFOLD

She had been a Playboy bunny, and rumor had it she had even been a centerfold. Paul wasn't as fascinated by the advent of this Swedish bombshell as his colleagues, but since he was the only unmarried member of the department, he could feel a general conspiracy gathering to bundle him somehow with the luscious summer presence. She was in town as an *au pair* for the Huntington children. The whole department was salivating, but it was a small college town, and they were all married. So, there was nothing for it but to pass along the lovely burden to Paul, their youngest and most callow colleague. They, of course, wished it could have been them, and were convinced that they would have handled the situation much better than poor Paul could ever do, but, given the circumstances, they all saw it as his collegial duty to pull himself together and be their standup guy, their representative in Congress, so to speak.

They took their turns. Beefy Neilson, the departmental jock, beads of sweat gathering on his brow, leaned into Paul's face, hoarse with intensity: "She's a real tomato, Paul, a real tomato, you know what I mean?" The word "tomato" was accompanied by a fine shower of spittle. It was clear he meant what he said. Darrell, on the other hand, sidling up to him, relied on a somewhat fuzzier metaphor as he murmured: "You know Paul, it's none of my business, but she's a real peach, a real peach. Think about it." Pudgy Melvin, who had written a monograph on Falstaff and who oversaw the departmental communal summer garden, whispered moistly into Paul's ear: "Wait till you see those boobs, man, they're like melons, I kid you not." Peter, always buffering life's setbacks with irony, simply said: "She'd be the apple of my eye, Paul, but alas, Jennifer would tear me apart, so what can I do? You, on the other hand...." The sentence hung in the air, and Paul felt the whole world gazing at him, as he hesitated before the time-worn, eternal cliché: *carpe diem*.

He still had not seen the girl from *Playboy*. Everyone else had, but he had been busy, now that the semester was over, finishing up his study on "The Hermeneutics of Distance in Tristan and Iseult." He hoped to present the paper at the annual conference of Comparative Medieval Studies just before the MLA next winter. In a shy way, he felt he had something new to say about the importance of distance, the importance of the horizon, where sky and sea seem to meet, just beyond all human reach. "Well," he said with a sigh, "I'll have to at least say hello, I suppose."

But before he could say hello, it was all arranged. Neilsen came bustling into his office, interrupting a delicate revision concerning the anxiety and heightened emotion provoked by the distance of the lover far off at sea, the other lover cocooned in a cave on land. "It's all taken care of," Neilsen chuckled. "We've reserved a canoe for you for late afternoon down at the boathouse. Gary, you know, the secretary's boyfriend, well, he's also in charge of the boathouse, he knows you're coming. Huntington will bring his babysitter down to the boathouse, and you can meet there. We agreed on seven-thirty, still plenty of light to find your way." Neilson's eyes were twinkling with vicarious delight. "Gary'll give you the key to the cabin on Treasure Island, you know where that is, don't you, down the river half a mile or so. Don't worry about a thing, it's all taken care of." Paul could feel dampness gathering under his arms. How unfortunate that none of his more enterprising colleagues were available for this adventure. "Thanks," he mumbled, "thanks a lot." The rising cadence at the end suggested at least a hint of irony, but Neilsen didn't mind. He clapped him on the shoulder, gave him a broad grin, and a thumbs up. Whistling cheerfully, he hurried down the corridor and out of sight.

Paul's revisions would have to wait. Since they were meeting at seven-thirty, he had to grab something to eat quite soon. He looked with regret at his manuscript, put a glass paperweight of a pink-clad skater in a globe of snowflakes on the page he was re-examining, took a light windbreaker from the hook on his door, and, almost like a condemned man leaving his cell, walked stolidly down the long, echoing hallway. He stopped downtown for a couple of slices of pizza, hardly a proper dinner, but he didn't have much of an appetite. He finished his beer, checked his watch, and saw that his time had come. With heavy steps, he returned to his car and drove the short distance down to the boathouse.

There was Huntington, snazzy as ever, fresh haircut, tweed jacket, impressive tan, even this early in the summer. Next to him stood his *au pair* girl for the season. "Elsa," Huntington made the introduction, "this is Professor Engelhart, you can call him Paul." And he turned from the willowy, tall blond, overtaxed, it seemed, by her well-formed bosom, to the youngest member of the department. "And

Paul, this is Elsa, Elsa Nordkvist, our marvelous *au pair* girl for the summer. I understand you will be canoeing on the river. Fine, fine. Well, now, I trust you will have a good time paddling around, and I am sure you will find lots to talk about." Turning to Elsa, he said encouragingly, "It may interest you that Paul here is writing on the importance of distance in the medieval romance, *Tristan and Iseult*." And, as he was turning to leave, he added: "By the way, it doesn't matter when Elsa gets back, as long as she's there to help us with breakfast at eight." Even Huntington, staid Huntington, seemed to have a twinkle in his normally guarded grey eyes, as he bent to enter his vintage Mercedes-Benz.

Paul was nervous, standing alone now with this formidable young woman, whom he still had not really met. She, however, seemed quite relaxed and ready for anything. He excused himself and went into the boathouse to get the key to the cabin on the Island. Gary, a huge smile plastered to his face, handed him the key attached to an oblong of wood painted green. And as he did so, he inserted a large packet of extra lubricated Trojan-super x condoms into Paul's other hand. "You never know when these might come in handy," he laughed, giving the young professor a clap on the back. "I figured a dozen should hold you." Paul flushed and felt dizzy. Stuffing the fat wad in his pocket, he mumbled his thanks and made his way outside. Together he and Elsa pulled a couple of lifejackets from the rack, picked up two slender wooden paddles, and carefully entered the canoe that had been reserved for them. When Elsa stepped down from the dock, the canoe tipped toward her and Paul, to steady her, took her arm, touching her for the first time. She laughed lightly, took her seat, picked up her paddle, and, together, almost in rhythm, they began to propel their craft out into the tranquil evening river.

It was the end of a pleasant June day, and the sun was dropping towards the pines on the far side of the river. The canoe cut through the dark water almost without a sound. Elsa seemed to have had some experience paddling in the past. In fact, Paul felt that the forward thrust of the canoe through the chill water was more the result of her stalwart effort than his own. It felt good on the quiet river and Paul would have been quite content, were it not for the unavoidable destination drawing implacably nearer with each deep stroke. The darkening river was empty, as if it had been reserved just for them. After about half an hour, a small pine-covered island rose through the blueish light. The canoe, as if with a will of its own, headed straight for the small wooden dock. They bumped against an old tire fender, grabbed a piling, and tied the canoe to a sturdy cleat. Elsa leaned over, her breasts swaying. He held out his hand, but she scrambled onto the dock without even noticing. He followed, envying Elsa her ease. The sun was starting to sink behind the trees and the sky was turning red. Paul would have been much happier if that neat little cabin had not been looming just down the wooden walkway. But there it was, and, without a choice, he followed her footsteps toward their destination.

The key entered the lock, the lock clicked, and the door, creaking on its hinges, swung open. They entered the dimness within the cabin. Elsa found an oil lamp and lit the flame. The cabin immediately felt welcoming, like a warm hearth, a shelter in the thickening dusk. How cozy it would have been, he reflected, if only he and Elsa were old friends. But she was a total stranger, and he felt paralyzed. She, on the other hand, flopped down on the soft old couch and drew him towards her. She clearly did not feel ill at ease. "Let me tell you about *Tristan and Iseult*," he offered, as she drew him in. She murmured, "Later," and pulled his head towards her soft and ample bosom. He fumbled with her pink blouse, he fumbled with his pants, he started fumbling with the string of a dozen condoms crammed in his pocket. She calmly removed her blouse and hung it over the back of the couch. She helped him unzip his jeans. With a pleasant chuckle, she took the strip of a dozen condoms from his trembling hand and detached the one at the end. "One at a time," she laughed. She opened the sealed packet and took out the extra lubricated Trojan-super x condom and said with a smile, "Can I help you?" He felt like a small frog about to be swallowed whole by a ravenous snake. She smiled again and, slipping the condom in place, started unrolling it. He lay there quivering. He was both aroused and appalled, and he wished he were back in his office working on his monograph. She shifted her body beneath him, and he felt that he was slowly being drawn into a mouth, a throat, a cave from which he would never escape. She eased him in, she caressed him, she made the proper movements, and despite his terror, he himself began to move. At that point, she suddenly whirled over, thrust him beneath her, and rose in all her statuesque beauty above him, illuminated by the warm glow of the oil lamp. She swayed back and forth, rose and settled, and despite his reluctance and doubt, they came, awkwardly, to something somewhat similar to what other people in such circumstances achieve.

Paul, however, felt annihilated. He felt ashamed. He knew he had not performed, that only Elsa had saved them from total defeat. But she said nothing, only murmured gentle sounds and stroked his face and chest. And he lay there, trembling like a rabbit, a mouse, a fool. After twenty minutes of silence, he tried to struggle to his feet, but she would not relinquish her position. "Don't you want to hear about that great medieval romance I'm working on?" he offered once again. "Later," she said," later," and her hand began to creep downwards. But now he burst forth, almost with violence, and freed himself from her grasp. He stood up, shaking. He quickly grabbed his underpants and his blue jeans and slipped them on. He stood above her voluptuous body, glowing white, like an alabaster statue, in the flickering illumination cast by the solitary lamp.

"I'm sorry, Elsa, I'm really sorry," he sobbed. "I can't do this, I just can't do this." For the first time, he tried to meet her eyes. "The problem is, how can I sleep with you when I don't even know you?"

Elsa looked at him, astonished, rose up, turned her back, and started pulling on her clothes. Once she was dressed, she finally spoke: "It's been years," she said, "since anyone even wanted to know me." They were dressed and ready to go. She blew out the oil lamp. Paul left the eleven super condoms on the side table for future, more enterprising visitors. They canoed back in silence. Paul wished he could find something comforting to say. He wished everything had been different. He wished he had known Elsa as a shy little child. He wished he had known her for years. But she had been a total stranger, an image projected by the fevered desire of his colleagues; she had never had a chance, and, as they approached the lights of the boathouse, he knew there was nothing he could say to make things right. And he knew he would never see her again.

DO YOU THINK HE LOVES ME?

She wasn't drop-dead beautiful, but she was pretty, bouncy, and gentle. She had sandy colored hair, a ponytail, and a happy little nose. Joseph found her pert looks and almost boyish, slender body surprisingly attractive. And she seemed to like him. A lot. Her name was Belinda. But as she said to him the very first day: "Just call me Belle, Honey. Everyone calls me Belle. It means beautiful, you know?"

It had started in Quito. He was shepherding thirteen students on a mid-winter biology expedition to the Galapagos. She was on the vacation of her life. Quito was just a stopover for all of them. As it turned out, Belinda was going to be a passenger on one of the two small sailboats his outfitter had leased for their two-week excursion amongst the islands. There had been an empty space in one of the boats, and the agency handling the arrangements was happy to squeeze in another passenger, another fare. He was delighted by this unexpected addition to his group.

Already in the pension in Quito, they were able to escape the curious and ironic glances of his students, who seemed to be everywhere. Alone in her room, they were lying quietly on top of her freshly starched sheets, the ceiling fan slowly swirling and streetlights flickering through the far window. An occasional drunken cry would rise from the cobblestoned street below. She was content after love, and she ran her fingernail slowly along his chest and gently over one of his nipples. When she began to talk, it was as if they had known each other for years, an old couple, comfortable in a sagging matrimonial bed. In a low, melodious voice, she spoke about the ordinary doings of her daily life.

"You know, Sweetie, I have a boyfriend back home in Vegas. His name's Ricky. Ah, hah. He was happy when he heard I won that casino lottery, but he thought it was dumb not to take the other trip they offered, the one to Paris, France. The Eiffel Tower and all that stuff, you know? I guess most gals would have gone for that, but not me. And you know why? Lemme tell you why. Ever since I was five years old, I've had a pet turtle, like my whole entire life, you know. I'll bet you can't guess what his name is, can you? Come on guess! Nah, you don't stand a chance. His name is Methuselah. Yup. That's from the Bible. A real old guy. I guess my turtle, who's getting a little bigger every year, might live forever with a name like that. So anyway, having a pet turtle my whole life, I'm really into turtles, you know what I mean? So, when the travel agency working with the casino showed me the brochures for the two trips I had to choose from, on one, there was the Eiffel Tower, sure, but on the other was a giant tortoise, ah hah, right there on the cover. For me it was a no-brainer, you know what I mean? I went for the giant tortoise! And here I am in bed with you in Quito and we haven't even got to the Galapagos yet. What do you think about that, Sweetie?" She kissed his ear and got back to her story.

"So, getting back to my boyfriend Ricky, he works at one of the best garages in town. He's a good mechanic, really. It comes in handy, you know? So it was my birthday last month, I'm a Sagittarius, I guess you could tell, you being a professor and all. Anyway, guess what happened. He picks me up at the Casino after work and insists on driving me home. I say what about my car in the parking lot and he says don't worry, we'll get it later, that's what he says. So he drives me home and stops in front of the house. We get out of the car and he wraps his arms around me and he says close your eyes and he steers me right up the driveway and stops, it feels like, right in front of the garage door. 'You got your door-opener?' he asks, in a mysterious tone of voice. I don't know what he's talking about 'No, I say, it's in my car down at the casino parking lot,' but then I feel something familiar slipping into my hand, and I guess what it is. So, not knowing what's going on, I press on the door-opener and listen to the creaky old door swinging up, all this with my eyes still shut. Then he says: 'Take a look, honey.' And what do I see? You'll never guess. There was my shiny Midnight Black V-6 Ford Mustang convertible, the real thing, which I got for $3,875, cuz the salesman liked me, he said. Well, I'll be paying good money on my monthly installments for the next six years, at least. But it's worth it, let me tell you. Ah ha. But here's the thing. 'Take a look at the tires, honey,' he says, nudging me forward. And you know what? You'll never believe it. There on my shiny Midnight Black V-6 Ford Mustang convertible were four swanky new whitewall tires and, for the life of me, I couldn't believe it. 'Happy Birthday, Honey,' he says with a big smile. 'Happy Birthday!' Can you imagine? He didn't just go and buy those beautiful whitewall tires that must have cost him a mint and have them delivered to my house. No way! What he did was this: he gave up his lunch hour, I know that's what he did, and, instead of eating, he snuck over to the casino parking lot, used the spare key I gave him just to show him that I trusted him, grabbed my car, drove to the garage, put my car up on the rack, got my old, worn down tires off and put them four swanky new whitewalls on, all by himself, lickety-split. Then he drove that car with its four new whitewalls to my house and used the garage door opener inside the car to open the garage so he could drive my car in, then shut the door. He must have had a friend from work drive along in a second car, so he could get back to the garage in time for the afternoon shift. I'll bet he didn't even get back in time and maybe they even docked him an hour's pay, but I hope not. So that's what he did!"

"He sounds like a nice guy," Joseph said in response to her long story.

Then she looked at him, still running her fingernail softly across his chest, and said, musingly, "I guess he must love me, don't you think? I mean, not just buying me those tires, but putting them all on by himself. Don't you think?"

"It sounds to me like he loves you," he assured her. She gave him a quizzical, but grateful look, then kissed him on the ear again, and they happily followed their instincts for a second time.

The two weeks in the Galapagos were spectacular. They had excellent guides who really knew the ropes. They visited beaches covered with sea lions and, at one point, Joseph came too close and had to flee for his life from a huge male defending his harem. The enormous bull, dripping in fat, was startlingly swift. A sumo wrestler who knew his business. His students couldn't stop laughing. Though it was against the rules, the next day, lithe Belinda rode briefly on the back of a giant land tortoise. She gave Joseph her Kodak, and he quickly snapped a few shots of her illicit ride. "Wait till Ricky sees those photos, he won't believe it," she said.

Also against the rules, one night a crew member dove down with a flashlight and a net and came back with enough lobsters for everyone. That very night, after dinner, an enormous thrashing could be heard in the bay. The guide said it must have been a huge manta ray trying to fight off an orca attack. The following morning, as they gathered on the beach, they saw a frantic splashing further out. A minute later a lone sea lion reached the shore. Where his hind flippers should have been, there were just two bleeding stumps, and he dragged himself along the sand toward a cave to die. Belinda was in tears. Joseph tried to comfort her, but generalizations about the cycle of life, about predators and prey, were of little use. The image of paradise had been punctured, and the sunshine didn't feel quite as warm as before, even to him.

***

For two weeks, Joseph and his students followed their guides, kept their journals, discussed Darwin, and soaked up sun and exotic otherness, far from their snow-covered campus back home. Belinda, despite the maimed little sea lion, was having the time of her life and was looking forward to showing Ricky her photos and telling him all about it when she got home. But part of her didn't want the adventure to ever end. As she said to Joseph, walking on a narrow path through the black volcanic rocks, "I don't think I'll ever get to another place like this again. I figure this is it. From now on, I guess it'll just be Vegas. I don't think Ricky's been further than the Grand Canyon." Joseph squeezed her hand and said he was sure she could convince Ricky to go on some exotic trip with her. "You think?" she replied, in a dubious tone of voice.

Living in tight quarters on the small sailboats, there was no chance for them to continue as lovers. But they remained friends and, once in a while, were able to wander off down the beach together for a few moments. Towards the end of the excursion, one afternoon, hidden from his students by some small sand dunes, they were able to share an embrace and a long kiss, a kind of seal on their time together and a prelude to good-bye. Belinda seemed anxious and Joseph held her gently to reassure her. Trailing her hand down his arm, Belinda said hesitantly: "You're really smart and all, so tell me, do you think Ricky really loves me? Do you think I should marry him, cuz I think maybe he's going to ask. What should I do?"

Joseph stood behind her and held her tight around the waist. He breathed in the clean smell from her sandy blond hair. He squeezed the muscles above her narrow shoulders, then leaned forward and kissed her gently on the temple. He had the feeling her question wasn't as simple as it sounded. He felt touched and uneasy. He drew in his breath, turned her round, and looked straight into her sky-blue eyes.

"Belle," he said, "you're a really good person, a real sweetie pie. Anyone who gets you is a lucky guy. It's obvious that Ricky loves you. And he should. When he proposes, and I'm sure he will, you should say 'yes.'"

He took her in his arms.

"Marry him, Belle," he breathed into her hair. And, almost believing his own words, he added: "I'm sure you'll be happy together for a long, long time."

SIMPLY REVENGE

For bodies understand each other. Souls do not.
Manuel Bandeira

Jurgen, Michael's uncle by marriage, aging and overweight, had suffered a massive stroke. But with characteristic tenacity, his fiercely loyal wife, Esther, had clung to his departing soul, had dragged it back against its will, had refused to allow it to follow its natural inclination. The flame was weary and tried to flicker its good-bye, but Esther was a tiger, and for the time being death didn't stand a chance.

Sheila was tall, slender, and impeccable in her starched white nurse's uniform. She was from Brisbane and in the midst of a two-year internship in the United States. With her blond tresses, deep tan, and long athletic limbs, she looked like a tennis player. She was Jurgen's principal nurse, and she did everything by the book. Her nurse's uniform swished as she walked and her rubber soles padded softly but firmly as she moved about the bed, recorded vital signs, then left the room and glided down the corridor.

Esther, still madly in love with her husband after forty-five years of sweetness and betrayals, imagined that everyone else was just as madly in love with him. And so she defended her man from all attacks, all possible beguilements, as he lay comatose in his hospital bed. She spoke to her *bubala* like a mother to her baby, almost cooing, though it was never clear that he could hear her. She tucked him in, put a cool glass of water to his lips, wiped carefully around his mouth and even on his chin. As she hovered over his bed, the nurses, once they had checked the vital signs and recorded the necessary statistics, tended to drift out of the room, leaving her, as she wished, totally in charge.

But finally, towards midnight, as silence filled the empty late-night corridors, she gathered up her things, murmured some final words of maternal adoration in her husband's ear, and taking hold of her nephew's strong arm, steered him out of the room, down the corridor, into the elevator, and then on to her comfortable old Mercedes 430 D in the parking lot. She was grateful to have the young man's presence at her side and to have him sitting behind the wheel. In fact, childless as she was, she loved her only nephew very much. However, it was natural that during this crisis there was little room in her heart for anything other than the all-consuming love of her life, her darling Jurgen, teetering on the edge between two kingdoms. Michael knew his aunt well and was simply content that his presence gave her some support. He didn't think Uncle Jurgen had much of a chance, but he also respected, in fact, was rather in awe of his aunt's fiery will. If anyone could pull him back from death's grasp, it was she.

On the way home, Aunt Esther sighed a good deal and murmured "My poor baby" many times. She also inveighed against the nurses, who, she said, were never good enough for her husband. She had a special antipathy towards Sheila, the nurse from Australia.

With that long-legged beauty from Down Under, she expected the worst.

"Did you see how she looks at my Jurgen, my poor baby, did you see? As if she wants to gobble him up. If they didn't make us leave at midnight, I would stay there till dawn to protect him. I can tell what she's thinking. But I won't let it happen. I will guard him no matter what."

Michael didn't know what to say. He was used to his dear aunt's highly emotive imaginings, but he didn't wish to offend her with a cold splash of reality. A fat old man, unconscious, living through machines, with a catheter in his penis, hardly a lady killer, hardly the man to entrance that young athletic Australian nurse in her impeccable white uniform. He put his arm around his aunt's shoulders and, as they floated silently down deserted El Camino Real, he took his eyes from the road for a second and hazarded a rapid kiss on her temple.

The next day, while Esther bent lovingly like a tiny willow over the hulk of her prostrate husband, Sheila gave Michael a look and headed for the corridor. Telling his aunt he was going for a Coke, he followed. They walked together down the corridor, moving away from his unfortunate uncle's room. Sheila started with a bit of candid, unprofessional small-talk.

"It looks as if he'll make it. The danger of another stroke is much diminished. But whether he will ever talk again, that's another question. In any case, you should take some comfort knowing your uncle is out of any immediate danger."

"Thank you for the good news," he replied. "Esther, as you can see, will do all she can to keep him in this world."

"Yes," Sheila replied, "she's a real tiger! I try to leave the two of them alone as much as possible."

"Yes, she's always been crazy about him. That's just the way she is."

"Well, he's lucky to have her, I suppose. In any case, may I change the subject? How about coming over to my place for a late dinner tonight? Then maybe a late-night movie on the tele?"

Michael was surprised and more than pleased. The week-long attendance at the bedside of his aunt's comatose husband was, in its daily monotony, quite exhausting. He could use a change. And Sheila, with her long limbs and brisk ways, would be a breath of fresh air. He nodded his thanks.

"How about meeting me out front at 10:15. I'm in a white Mustang."

"Great. OK. See you then," and he turned to rejoin his indefatigable aunt in her bedside vigil.

"Aunt Esther," he began. "You don't mind driving home without me this evening, do you? I really think I need to take some time off, relax, maybe go to a late movie. You just take the car and someone will give me a ride." And then, spurred by hopeful imaginings, he added, "If I don't come home tonight, I'll just meet you here at the hospital again tomorrow, OK, auntie?"

"Fine, my darling, fine. I understand very well. But where," and she gazed at him with European amusement, "where's your Coca-Cola?"

"Oh, yes, the Coke! Well, I was so thirsty I drank it down right beside the machine."

"I'm sure you were very thirsty, darling," she responded, and gave him a playful hug.

The afternoon and evening dragged on. Bubala remained with his eyes closed, but his regular breaths lifted his crisp white sheet, then let it drop back down. Michael read through three issues of *National Geographic*, brought his aunt a coffee and a raspberry Danish, her favorite, he knew, and consulted his watch. Finally, it was almost ten o'clock.

"OK, auntie, I think I'm going to take off, maybe catch a late show at the Guild Theater or grab a coffee and check out the book display over at Kepler's. You'll be OK, won't you?" and, lightly patting the shoulder of his unconscious uncle, he stepped back, embraced his aunt, and kissed her on the cheek.

"See you tomorrow, then," she said, with cheerful irony. Aunt Esther was a bit of a hysteric, but she was also a woman of the world. She knew how things worked. She knew that Kepler's closed at five and the last show at the Guild was at 8. She also knew that the Coke machine in their corridor had been out of commission all day. But none of that mattered, since, after her beloved *bubala*, her darling nephew was the apple of her eye. And Michael, embarrassed by his fumbling attempts at subterfuge, felt safe, nonetheless, in the embrace of her love.

Out front, the white Mustang emerged from the dark. He slipped in and, with a small roar, they were off. The evening was chilly, and Sheila had pulled a cashmere sweater over her nurse's uniform. He wanted to touch the soft wool but restrained himself. After all, he hardly knew her.

After a thrown-together dinner of cold cuts, salad, and a nicely chilled gazpacho soup, accompanied by a Merlot from Napa Valley, they moved to the living room and sat on the couch facing the T.V. As Sheila finished her third glass of Merlot, she yawned, stretched, and said to Michael "It's been a long day at work, I'm really tired, perhaps instead of the tele we can go to bed? How would that be?"

He gulped down the last of his wine, got to his feet, put his arm over her shoulder and said not a word. She glided toward her bedroom on the same silent rubber soles that served so well in the hospital corridors. He glided along, as best he could, in his beige hush puppies.

And then he was in bed with a stranger. Her sheets were cool and clean, her legs were long and tawny from the California sun, and her blond hair spread like a halo on her pillow. He was not accustomed to going to bed with strangers, but the half bottle of Merlot and her healthy young breasts and perfect flat stomach conspired to make things easier. She clasped him by the neck, pulled him down, pressed her lips to his, and pulled him inside her. They made love and, just before drifting off, he thought stupidly of Frank Sinatra's "Strangers in the Night." Then he was gone, and she was already gone, and left behind were two contented bodies lying side by side.

Coming awake three hours later, he felt that lithe athletic shape stretched warm beside him. Light from the streetlamp outside was seeping through the slats of her venetian blinds, painting stripes on her slender, slumbering body. He watched her breasts softly rise and fall, like the gentle surge of the sea in a protected cove. He reached out and ran his fingers down her side. She rolled sleepily toward him and, eyes still shut, pouted her lips. They kissed, then kissed some more, and Michael, who had majored years before in Classics, thought this time of Catullus, rather than Frank Sinatra. They wrapped their arms around each other and once again made love. But this time, he felt as if he knew her, or at least as if he wanted to know her. And then they drifted off into oblivion again.

He awoke to the smell of coffee and English muffins, and he thought he was in love. He brushed his teeth in the bathroom with his fingers, then stumbled into the kitchen. He draped an arm over Sheila's shoulders and tried to kiss her on the lips. Already dressed in her immaculate nurse's uniform, she squirmed away and gave him a peck on the cheek. "Eat your brekki," she said in her brisk nurse's tone. He slumped onto one of the kitchen chairs and picked up his cup of coffee, blowing on it gingerly. He added sugar and took a few sips. He crunched on his nicely buttered English muffin. He was finally ready to speak.

"That was great, Sheila. No, not the English muffin, I mean that was good, too, but I mean the night. I felt we got closer during the night, don't you think? I mean, I really was starting to, starting to, well, really like you. A lot." And after an awkward pause, he added, "Can we get together again tonight?" He gazed at her with puppy dog eyes. But she had turned away to attend to the last dishes from the previous evening. Without looking at him, she said, "I'm sorry, Michael, it was all very nice. You're very good in bed. It was all a bloody ripper. But I'm afraid we can't go on. We simply can't."

He was stunned. "Why not," he quavered.

"Because, my dear," and here she did turn around to face him directly, "my fiancé is returning from the East Coast tonight."

"Your fiancé," he foolishly repeated. "You have a fiancé? You're going to get married?

"Well, as a matter of fact, we are. That son-of-a-bitch."

Bewildered, he went on: "But why did you invite me over, why did you sleep with me?"

"Well," she said, and there was a long pause. "You're a good-looking chap and I knew my fiancé was betraying me in New York with his ex-girlfriend, and I was furious." She walked over, put her slender, capable hand on his arm, and said, "Listen up, mate, you're a lovely fella, but last night, my sweet, last night," and she paused for a moment, "last night you were simply revenge." And then she added, as if in wry consolation, "Don't worry, I'll tell him we did it three times."

Michael took another sip of coffee, but it had turned lukewarm and tasted like nothing at all. Mechanically, he crunched the last bit of English muffin between his teeth and forced himself to swallow. His eyes were glued to the tabletop.

"Shall we go, luv," Sheila called out briskly, picking up her handbag and striding towards the door. Michael followed without a word, and slid into the front seat beside her, like any suburban husband proud that his wife was doing the driving. As they rolled toward the hospital, he suddenly realized how very much he was looking forward to embracing his feisty, worldly, sentimental and fiercely romantic Aunt Esther. He knew he would find her hovering at the bedside of her beloved, comatose husband, whom she would protect from all other women, especially nurses in white, and never, never allow to die.

BENEATH THE BOUGAINVILLEA OF FOLEGANDROS

On many Greek islands, visitors remain in the port, where they sit in cafes and bars, drink ouzo, nibble at dolmades, dip pita bread into tzatziki yogurt mix, and gaze out at the boats anchored in the harbor, all facing the wind as they swing on their anchor chains. Then they stroll to the adjacent beach, take a swim in the warm, crystal-clear water, apply lotion to their pale limbs, and, beginning to fry in the summer heat, flip their way through a magazine or a newspaper picked up in Athens, just before they mounted the ferry in Piraeus. Once their shoulders have begun to grow pink, they arise, gather up towel and reading matter, and return to their favorite restaurant to share a bottle of retsina, as if drinking sap straight from the pine, followed by an enormous fresh fish with goggle eyes or dripping lamb shish kebabs.

But on Folegandros, the port was nothing but a pier and the nearby beach merely adequate. The real life on the island was to be found uphill at the Chora, a good hour climb from the sea. There were several squares in the Chora, all pleasantly dappled with shade from willowy lime trees and spreading bougainvillea trellised above the patios of the white-washed bars and restaurants that line each street. Because the Chora was distant from the sea, one felt more intimately at home on the island, as if the absence of touristic beach and the ferry that brought one there and carried one away allowed for a more genuine relationship to the otherness of the small island world. It may have been an illusion, of course, but somehow, lazily seated in the shade, listening to the shrill mechanical cry of invisible cicadas, fingering a cool glass of cloudy ouzo, with the sticky taste of licorice on one's tongue, one felt less a tourist passing through, and more a human being in a good and human place.

It was in one of those orderly clean squares that I met a young couple from Athens. When the beautiful girlfriend with her enormous green eyes and languid dancer's body arose to freshen up in the lady's room, I turned from my table to face the young man and posed my usual question. "Do you speak English? Good. May I ask, do you play chess?" His eyes lit up and he smiled. I held out my small portable magnetic set, but he shook his head, lifted his palm to gesture "wait," and disappeared inside the restaurant. A moment later he returned, carrying a green and white roll up board and a heavy walnut box, with time-worn weighted wooden pieces nestled within. They felt smooth and solid to the hand. We exchanged names and aligned our forces before his girlfriend could return. We were well into a Sicilian Defense by the time she appeared. She merely smiled, as if accustomed to such interludes, and, taking a seat at an adjacent table, immersed herself in a celebrity movie magazine.

I nodded hello to her, said *Yiassou*, one of my few Greek words, then turned back to the game. Her boyfriend played well. He was attentive and cautious, perhaps too much so. We were evenly matched for about an hour, but then the tide began to favor me. As my mating net tightened, he pondered the situation, contemplating the complexity and its implications. After five minutes of silence, he looked up, smiled, and, with a charming accent, gently said, "I resign." We shook hands and agreed to meet again the next day in mid-afternoon. He went inside to return the house chess set. While he was gone, his girlfriend held up her magazine opened to a photo of Angelina Jolie. "Andzelina Zoli," she said, with a broad smile and a blinding flash of white teeth, holding the portrait of the movie star next to her own face. She pointed at the Hollywood beauty and at herself and laughed. "Andzelina–Angeliki," she said. She had great green eyes, long flowing ash-blond hair, a strong nose. When she spoke, it was always Greek, and its sound was filled with mystery and exotic promise. In truth, she looked a lot like Angelina Jolie.

Our chess games were so rewarding that I ended up prolonging my stay on Folegandros. It was hard to imagine abandoning the pleasant, shaded town square with its hibiscus and bougainvillea on all sides, its cobbled streets, its white-washed facades. We played every afternoon, and we always enjoyed our struggles. And then one day, after I had lingered on the island for a full week, Geórgios finally found his best game. Cramped on my queenside by an uncomfortably passive French Defense, my white bishop blocked forever by my own stupid, stolid pawn structure, I watched as the white pieces marshalled themselves for a concerted kingside attack. I surveyed my position, hopelessly blocked like midtown traffic in New York. With a constricted heart, I searched for a way out, for exchanges to simplify, to lead toward an endgame in which I could draw. But there was nothing to be done. I glanced over Geórgios' shoulder at Angeliki, her green eyes flickering over the pages of her movie magazine. I sighed and reached across the table. "Congratulations," I said. "That was an elegant game you just played." We both smiled. We were both glad.

But that game seemed to be a sign, and that night I finally packed my bags, ready to move on. The next day, Geórgios and his girlfriend accompanied me to the ferry that would eventually bring me, via other stops, to Amorgos. As I shook hands goodbye and clasped the Greek's arm with warmth, again my gaze was drawn to the huge green eyes of Angeliki just behind him, eyes that called to me like fathomless wells of crystal-clear water. *Yassou* I said to the chess player and his green-eyed beauty. And suddenly I realized why it had been so hard to leave that wonderful island, why I had lingered, almost transfixed, for an entire week or even more, for I had lost count of the days. And with my hand still gripping Geórgios' arm, I stared into the sparkling green depths of Angeliki's eyes for the last time. *Yassas*, I said, using the respectful form worthy of a goddess. As I reached down for my bags, she gazed back for a moment. She nodded, smiled, and clearly understood everything.

CHESS ON NAXOS

For Lena

I love Greek islands. I have been to seventy-four of them. The biggest was Crete, the smallest had no name, and in an hour, I swam around it.

I do not speak Greek, but I love the sound of it. Just listen to the music of the encircling Cyclades: *Makronissos* (where I have never been), *Kea* (forgive me, the only island I have forgotten), *Kithos, Serifos* (where I slept in an Orthodox church hostel on a monk's bed hard as a stone), *Sifnos, Milos* (where my teenage son learned fifty words a day for his SATs), *Folegandros* (where a young disk jockey drove himself, with two Danish girls, over the cliff late one exuberant night), Andros (where I defeated the local cook who had been Greece's Junior Chess Champion fifteen years before), *Tinos, Mykonos* (where, in 1964, I slept like an angel on the beach, enveloped in a youth that will never come again), *Delos* (where no one could spend the night, but where tourists would arrive in flocks all day), *Paros* and tiny *Anti-Paros* (with its dark and unexpected cave), *Ios* (famous for discos, so I never went), *Sikinos, Thira* (*Thera* to classicists, *Santorini* to hordes of young backpackers), *Donousa*, *Amorgos* (where I lived in a mountain village with my son, by then out of college, and where he stayed on to write in that quiet, unknown village an hour's walk on steep trails to the nearest beach), and *Anafi,* where I still hope, someday, to go.

Almost in the middle of that lovely mix of stony islands, sprinkled with houses like white cubes of bright sugar beneath the Mediterranean sun, stone houses of fresh whitewash accentuated by blue shutters and trimming, lies Naxos, famous for its classical ruins, its mountain peak, Mt. Zas or Mt. Zeus, the highest in the Cyclades, and its splendid beaches and gracious mountain villages. It is on Naxos that this very brief chess story occurs.

My woman friend at the time was a Brazilian ballerina. We had a lot in common. We were both in love with her body. I remember waking one morning to see her quietly sitting on the edge of our bed, slowly turning her arm to the left, then to the right, gazing steadily at what, clearly, even now in retirement, was a work of art, her own *chef d'oevre*. She was happy whenever we were alone, but uncomfortable whenever others threatened the harmonious simplicity of our bubble. We had already been in Greece for a couple of weeks, and her finely tuned, delicately firm body had grown from something close to alabaster to its present healthy, sun-filled radiance.

I had just stepped out for a brief stroll and had encountered a young man on the deck of his downstairs apartment. I had inquired if he would like to play chess sometime, and he had replied in the affirmative. "How about later this afternoon," he suggested. Sounded good to me.

I trotted up the stairs to our own apartment, half bright with sunlight, half sequestered in grateful shade.

"Darling," I proclaimed. "Guess what?" Her green eyes sparkled.

"What's up?" she said in colloquial Portuguese. English was not part of her cultural heritage. I was happy enough, for I loved her Carioca accent, that flavor of Rio de Janeiro she carried with her at all times. It was like a tropical fragrance, melding with her perfect body.

"I'm so lucky, honey. I found a guy who wants to play chess!"

"Oh, that's marvelous!" she replied. "Just what you were looking for. I'm so happy for you, my love."

"Yes, it will be great to have a few chess games. And it's so convenient, the guy's right downstairs in our own unit."

"Wonderful. Come and give me a kiss."

I leaned over and kissed her, for she was, after all, the princess of my life.

"So," she went on, after removing her soft, moist lips from mine, "so when do you think you guys will get a chance to play?" She had a gentle smile on her flawless, classical face, balancing delicately above her ballerina's slender but sturdy neck.

"Well, as a matter of fact, I'm really lucky. He says he is available later this afternoon."

"This afternoon?" It was as if a cloud, rare in the summer sky of the Aegean, had passed over the sun. "This afternoon?" Her smile was gone.

"Anything wrong with that?" I asked, but my heart was already constricting.

"This afternoon? So soon? No, I don't think that is a good idea at all. Not at all!"

Needless to say, Gregorio and I didn't play chess that afternoon, nor did we play that evening. In fact, we never played a single game, and all I could do was go down, apologize, and point sheepishly upstairs in explanation. Gregorio understood and gave me a sad look and a slap on the back. "That's life," he said, in heavily accented English.

This is a very short story about chess on Naxos. A story that never occurred.

But boy was she beautiful.

SAGRES

Surf came rolling in, crystal clear, icy cold. Richard and his new friend Jake had to force themselves to stride out through the swirl and tug, dive through a cresting breaker, do a wild crawl for twenty seconds, then dive through another onrushing wall of foaming water, feeling all the time the burn of the Atlantic's icy grip on their skin. They would dive, ride the waves, exult, leap up, cry out, and feel foolishly, utterly, triumphantly alive. Emerging finally from the ocean, they would be tingling with life in every pore. It was a great beach for the young, and Jake, at least, was young.

After leaving the water, they would run down the hard-packed sand beneath the towering orange cliffs, then back again, drying off in the ocean breeze and warmed by the vertical summer sun. Returning to their towels, they would flop down, split open an orange, munch on some almonds, and drink from their still sweating cans of Sumol. Then Richard would snap open his magnetic chess set and, shifting gears, they would begin to play. Richard could see that Jake was better, but only a little better, so they both immersed themselves in the game and had the pleasure of mortal combat. Usually, after a lengthy battle, Jake would win, but once in a while, Richard would find himself with the extra pawn and a winning endgame. It turned out that his partner, his rival, was first board back at the Cal Berkeley chess club. A stronger player, he was also taller than Richard, slender and good-looking. Richard had always been proud of his dark summer tan, but he ruefully noticed that Jake's tan had a deeper resonance of robust health. And, of course, he himself was already *nel mezzo del cammin di nostra vita*, hairline beginning to recede, waist slowly beginning to thicken. Despite the contrast, however, hanging with Jake felt good, as his blood rose to a remembrance of days past and he wrestled his body back to the vigor of youth.

He had first discovered this beach of demanding purity fifteen years earlier and had been coming back ever since. The cliffs, the waves, the wind, remained the same. So, too, the youngsters on the beach, or so it seemed. In fact, during the unrolling of those years, the only thing that had changed had been Richard himself. Sagres remained a living photograph, a kind of miracle. It never aged. The kids on the beach never aged. Only he was caught, wriggling in the fisherman's net of time.

It was an idyllic existence, but, of course, it couldn't last. Every year, he would spend the last two weeks of summer in Sagres, and every year, he would have to tear himself away, packing up just in time to catch the afternoon bus for Lisbon, leaving paradise to the eternally young. He was a professor and had to fly home to begin the fall semester. The others were unencumbered by outside reality, or so it seemed to him. In any case, this particular summer, the forced departure was even more painful than usual. For this was the summer in which, at the last moment, Pascale turned up. And time held its breath.

They first saw her coolly downing an afternoon beer at the Dromedario as they passed by on their way to the beach. She looked a bit older than the usual crowd, eyes sparkling blue-green, as if drawn straight from the sea. One glimpse of her, and all Richard could do was swallow. He looked at Jake and could see it was the same for him. But they kept on walking, made it to the beach, and did their usual thing. The ocean was as transparent as ever, its sting as sharp as always. They ran the hard-packed sand left by the receding tide, flopped down on their towels, split open an orange, shared their almonds, gripped their still-cool cans of Sumol, and joined combat once again in that infinite realm hidden within sixty-four squares. The crashing of the waves, the chatter of little children building sandcastles, the occasional piercing cry of a gull, all receded as, entering the accustomed field of battle, growing enmeshed in the usual agony, they began to test and probe, seeking weaknesses, like wary wrestlers circling the mat. Two hours later, as was almost predictable, Richard resigned. They took another swim, dried off with another run, then headed up to town together.

As they passed through the oblong square with its open-air bars, there she was, calmly sipping a coffee and eating a Danish. They took the next table, ordered a couple of beers, and introduced themselves. She flashed glistening white teeth and replied with a charming French accent, "Je m'appelle Pascale, I am Pascale." She gazed at them with eyes like the translucent waves of the sea and as piercing as the ocean's icy freshness. She sat there, trim, quiet, confident, in a well-cut white beach blouse, a floppy white hat jaunty on her head. "It's good here, is it not?" she said, tapping her *Gauloise* on the edge of the seashell ashtray. She looked at them both through a puff of smoke and her eyes, old with wisdom, but dancing with amused vitality, narrowed and seemed to lock on like radar. Somehow her banal words felt like a challenge, but all Richard could manage was a pleasant platitude, "Best place in the world."

Her lips were finely etched, her cheeks were high, her forehead broad, her blond hair a tangle somehow at peace beneath the straw hat perched on its nest. She talked about Paris, about Cap Ferrat, about her travels in Spain. "I have come here because it is the end of the world, n'est-ce pas?" she said through another puff of mesmerizing smoke, narrowing her eyes once again. Struck almost mute by her presence, Richard and Jake simply nodded in agreement. It was indeed the end of the world, the final jumping off point. Nothing beyond but the icy beauty of the endless Atlantic, cresting and breaking, spreading spume in the air and foam on the beach.

"Well," she said, "it is time for my afternoon nap. Perhaps we shall meet at the Dromedario tonight?" She crushed her last cigarette in the seashell, stood up, gestured to the waiter, paid her bill, and strode off, her white, free-flowing dress swirling around her. Jake took a last pull on his beer. Richard sat there stunned, then said, "Wow!"

After dinner, the chess partners wandered down towards the harbor and listened to the clinking of the rigging on the sailboats swaying in the evening breeze down below. They got an ice cream at the last kiosk, then made their way back towards the brightness before the Dromedario. The street was filled with the usual overflow of the young and eager. They pushed their way inside, got a beer each, then looked around. Pascale was at a corner table, speaking French. They grinned and nodded to her, and, surprisingly, she excused herself and came to them. "My compatriots," she said, gesturing to the table. They went outside and stood in the milling crowd with the attentive seagulls on its edges. Richard picked up a French fry from the ground and threw it, but before it could land, a seagull had fluttered up to grab it midair. They chatted about the beaches, Jake told them about surfing down at Santa Cruz, back home in California. Pascale said she hoped to see more of the coast before heading home to France. Richard then surprised even himself.

"My summer is coming to an end. Tomorrow's my last day in Sagres. I'm going to rent a scooter and go up the coast to the beaches around Carrapateira." He hazarded a quick glance at her face. "Want to come along?" He couldn't believe his sudden temerity. Jake gave him a funny look and smiled. Pascale paused, took a last drag on her *Gauloise*, threw the butt down, crushed it into the ground with a circular motion, and, gazing off into the night, said with a slow smile, "Pourquoi pas?" After some more chit-chat, Pascale said, "Et alors, demain, ici, how about ten o'clock, yes?" and with a smile, she took her leave and returned to the round table of her compatriots.

The next morning Richard was there in front of the Dromedario with his scooter and a small knapsack laden with sandwiches, fruit, and a bottle of wine. Pascale showed up with the floppy white hat, a very short skirt, and a luxurious silk scarf calculated to complement her eyes. They went inside, ate a breakfast of yogurt topped with granola and strawberries, then set off on their adventure up the coast.

As they rode out of town, Richard could hear her hat flopping in the wind, as she tightened her grip around his waist. He could feel her fingernails through his light summer shirt. They made their way to Vila do Bispo, then took the old dirt road to the lonely beach at

Cordoama, where they settled beneath the pulsating heat of the friable orange cliffs and strolled through the foamy shallows between the
beach and the seven rows of breakers rolling in. Back at their towels,
they had a snack and she looked out at him from beneath the shelter
of her silky blue-green scarf. He should have kissed her, but he didn't
dare.

Back on the scooter, they returned to Vila do Bispo, then took the
main road north through pine barrens towards Carrapateira. Before
getting there, they branched off on the sandy road to Amado. It was
already late September, so they found the beach deserted. They settled
down and watched the heavy surf breaking and rolling toward them,
powerful, eternal, beautiful, indifferent. They ate their sandwiches
hiding from the wind, within the gossamer penumbra of her blue-
green scarf. They drank the bottle of Dão. On the wind-swept, naked
beach, they lay close together, and Richard gathered enough courage
to kiss her sun-warmed shoulder. She lazily rolled over and brushed
her mouth across his lips. She tasted of salt, and he felt grains of sand
on his tingling lips.

As the sun dropped in the sky, they gathered up their things
and returned to the scooter. Again, she wrapped her arms around his
waist, and her fingernails dug into his flesh. Richard knew what he
had to do and, when they passed a solitary structure advertising
rooms, he pulled in. The owner looked as if he had been napping.
"No," he said, "Keine Zimmer, no rooms, season over. Fechado. Finished. Schluss," and he turned away and closed his door. Feeling like
a fool, Richard got back on the scooter, Pascale tightened her grip, and
they rode home through the chill evening breeze. He could have gone
north to seek a room in Carrapateira, but he did not. He could have

stopped off in Vila do Bispo, but he did not. Defeated, he drove back to Sagres, kissed her goodbye on the cheek in front of the Dromedario, and, disconsolate, drove back to his hotel.

**

A few years later, Richard found himself, once again in late summer, on his favorite beach. And to his surprise, there was Jake, smiling and deeply tanned. "Jake," he exclaimed, and the men embraced. "How's it going, Jake?"

"Great. I'm half-way through grad school now. Marine Biology. I spend a lot of time at the labs down at Monterrey. And still go surfing up at Santa Cruz. Say, did you hear? A guy up at Santa Cruz got eaten by a Great White. His board came floating in three days later with this jagged cookie-cutter hunk missing. They never found his body."

They spread their beach towels beside each other and lay there soaking in the afternoon sun. Then Jake rolled over and said, "Remember that sexy Pascale we both liked a few years ago? She was something else. A bit old for me, but you know, an older French woman knows her way around. Anyway, as it turned out, a week after you left, we went hitch-hiking together all the way from Sagres to Paris. She flagged down all the rides, of course, in her white miniskirt, those long, tanned legs. We took our time: down the Algarve, over to Seville, Cordoba, Granada, great place Granada, down to Barcelona, through the Pyrenees, then through Carcassonne, another great place, then up to Angoulême, Poitiers, the Loire, Orleans, Chartres, and finally Paris. Great trip. Good old Pascale, with that sensuous silk scarf, remember? Boy, did she like to laugh. We had a really good time. She was the greatest!"

And once again Richard felt how Jake, indeed, was the better man, and all he could do, brimming with jealousy, was smile, clap him on the back, and say: "Good man!" And after gazing off into the distance for a bit, they returned to the present. Richard snapped open his trusty traveling set, laid down the black and white metallic board, shuffled two pawns behind his back, then held out his fists. Jake nonchalantly slapped his left hand and, as one might have predicted, he had chosen white. Richard smiled and prepared to defend himself. "Perhaps I'll play the French this time," he thought with a wry smile, "in memory of Pascale." But, though the game had not yet begun, he felt strangely weary and quite sure of what the result would be.

NORWEGIAN BUTTERFLY

For A-M

Her husband was a good guy. Having met Kristina on vacation, he had given up a promising career as a botanist in Germany in order to live with her in the far reaches of Norway's rugged west coast. I would have done the same. You would have, too.

Every morning, there came a gentle tap on my window, and there she was, slender as a reed, smoking her eternal cigarette (this happened decades ago, of course), welcoming me into the new day. I would jump up, pull on a bathing suit, brush my teeth, stuff a beach towel, a magnetic chess set, a sandwich, and a can of cold soda into my backpack, then dash out to join her and my chess partner, her husband. They had driven down from Norway in their small car, and we had developed a pattern of going each morning to a distant, endless stretch of sand that could only be reached by a long and dusty dirt road. The beach was called Cordoama, and it was a few miles from the modest district capital of Vila do Bispo, near the southwestern tip of Europe. It was the most beautiful beach I had ever encountered in Europe. There were always seven ranks of breaking waves rolling steadily towards the shore, and body surfing was always good. Behind the wide white sand loomed enormous friable reddish-brown cliffs, pulsing with the heat of the day. The beach was almost deserted because it was hard to get to, and, except for a single modest restaurant, there were no facilities.

At the time, I was still a runner, but nothing like them. The beach was vast and went on for miles. It was so gently sloped that it seemed utterly flat, especially when the tide was out. We would go for a long run, then examine tide pools at the base of steep cliffs that dropped straight down to the ocean. On the way back, her husband would give us both an enormous head start, but no matter how far ahead we were, he would always catch us before we reached our backpacks and towels, where we had established our home base beneath the reddish cliffs.

Our vast stretch of sand was considered a nudist beach, but I wore my bathing suit with my usual American modesty. In those days, did the expression "uptight" already exist? In deference to the middle-aged American university professor, Kristina did not strip down completely but wore only her bikini bottom, a delicate strip of black ribbon, clinging precariously to the edges of her pelvic girdle, lightly grazing her childlike hips and flat underbelly. I am convinced that that thin strip of almost gauzy silk intensified her beauty with a suggestion of nudity beyond any dimension that true nakedness could have achieved. To this day, I remember my mother's witty poetic repost to this aspect of the human condition:

"Why does nude rhyme with lewd
and naked (almost) with sacred?"

Her husband, in terrific, slimmed-down, long-distance runner's shape, wore a green Speedo so dark that from an angle it, too, looked black. I wore my usual blue-and-green bathing trunks, boxer-style, of course. And we all swam. And rode the waves. And he and I played chess.

Helmut was good. In addition to being a fine cross-country runner, he was a cultured and intelligent young man. But he was trapped in the boondocks of western Norway, far from the high culture of Germany in which he had grown up. He felt very cut off, very alone. Of course, after years of marriage to Kristina, he spoke decent Norwegian, but there was scarcely anyone to talk to except for her. It isn't so easy for a man rich with the cultural wealth of a fallen world to return to the simple joys of mere Eden. Yet it was easy to see how he had been compelled to make that choice.

About the chess on Cordoama, when I think back, I must admit I cannot remember winning or losing. I know the games were well-contested and interesting, but no openings, variations, blunders, or brilliant strategies survived. All I remember is a black silken butterfly flitting around the edges of our chess board, doing a bit of Yoga, climbing a short way up the friable cliff face, searching for unusual shells, for fossils in the rock, trotting down to the water and back, always on the edge of my vision, on the edge of that safe and orderly world tucked into sixty-four black and white squares, a world where chance and the alure of the irrational were kept at bay.

I have changed her name to save you from a fruitless journey to the west coast of Norway. She and her husband have been divorced for many years now, but, as is the way of this world, even Kristina is well into middle age by now. Cordoama you can find almost unchanged, but the Kristina of my memory will not be there. The beauty of chess is eternal, unlike the grace of human flesh. Unless...

MELÚ

James had been gazing, with his usual sense of wonder and exhilaration, at the endless unfurling of the surf, when he noticed someone far out, riding the crest of a distant wave. Most people at this wild beach bathed close to shore. Even teenagers rarely went further than the nearest line of crashing breakers. Real surfers with their boards never came to this beach, but clustered in large numbers at the crescent-shaped cove just a kilometer away, where the curving sands created a smooth and deep swell, perfect for a long and gentle ride. Yet here, in this waning afternoon, there was a body, a someone, melded with the frothing distant rollers, effortlessly advancing with the water's rush. He shaded his eyes and seemed to make out a mass of yellow hair streaming behind the gliding figure, drawing slowly closer. Now the figure had mounted a swell only three ranks out and was drawing ever closer. The gliding body was a woman, a creature clearly at home in the freshness of the open Atlantic, as it came pounding rhythmically towards the bright sand beach, a swimmer at play in the surging blue fields of the Lord.

Now she had risen on a new swell, only two ranks away, inexorably gliding forward, as if part and parcel with the incoming tide.

Mesmerized, James rose to his feet and gingerly hopped down the still-hot sand toward the shallows. There were tiny minnows floating to and fro with the gentle eddies of crystalline water lapping the shore. The wet sand felt good on the soles of his feet. He gazed out to sea, and there she was, having somehow slipped from the roiling third range of breakers to the second, seemingly without lifting an arm, without taking a stroke. He watched as her body rose with a gathering crest, then glided down the foaming slope, coming closer and closer. And then she was caught up in the last row of roiling surf, flowing towards where he stood in the knee-deep glittering shallows.

Her slender body floated almost to his feet, where she finally beached herself. She didn't stand up, but lay there in the glittering afternoon tide, quiet and content. Like many on this stretch of beach, she wore no bikini top, but she seemed to be wearing a kind of wet suit up to her waist, a wet suit that shimmered blue and green as she swayed with the water swirling round his feet. She looked up at James through fathomless green eyes, smiled, and addressed him.

"Would you like to ride some waves with me," she said, as if the salutatory norms of initiating a conversation with a stranger were irrelevant to her. James was a traveler and had pursued linguistics in grad school, but her accent was hard to place, not quite French, certainly neither Spanish nor Portuguese. Like a somnambulist, James heard himself reply: "Yes, let's go and ride some waves," as if it were the most normal proposition in the world. "I'm Jim," he offered, as he started to stride towards deeper water, while she, without rising, turned gracefully around and drifted, like floating algae, back towards the open sea. "Jeeem", she repeated, in melodious acknowledgement. "Melú," she added, as if in an afterthought, and the final vowel stretched forth, like a prolonged note from a flute, gently wavering toward the distant horizon.

Moving in a dream, James dove through the breakers, swam underwater, and pushed steadily away from shore. Sooner than he would have imagined, they had reached the seventh row of breakers, after which there was nothing but open sea. The swimmer who had come from beyond the surf continued to glide around him, comfortable in her element. She started to move further away from shore, but James, shaking off his spell, said, "No, this is good here, from here we can ride the waves back." She gave him a quizzical look, but simply said, "OK." Even those two syllables, the prolonged initial vowel, the clipped voiceless stop that followed, seemed to come from some distant language James had never encountered before. Were there remnants of Celtic still spoken hereabouts? Were fragments of Manx, Cornish, Gallaecian, still extant in obscure villages at the end of unnamed dirt tracks? It was a mystery. When he asked her where she was from, Melú seemed not to hear and dove into the gurgling froth of a breaking wave.

And so they rode the mounting swells of the seventh range of waves, crystal-clear, stinging cold, filled with a freshness of affirmation. They rode in, then returned, rode in, then returned, remaining always at the same distance from shore. His companion said nothing and James, enthralled by her and by the sea, was content to float in his senses. But finally, growing cold, he turned to her and said: "Let's go back, OK?" A shadow crossed her face and, in a soft voice, she replied, "Already?" Again, he noticed that indefinable accent and sensed the deep allure of otherness.

"Let us continue to ride these perfect waves, these endless waves," she pleaded in her soft and distant way. Her English was perfect, even refined, but certainly it was not her native tongue. For James, her voice still held a mysterious appeal, but the pleasant sting of the cold water had lost its attraction. In fact, he felt it was penetrating his very bones.

"But aren't you getting cold?" he asked. Her body continued to drift, to hover, to slip gently around him. In fact, she looked perfectly content out there where the surge turned to breakers that began their long roll toward the distant beach. He was amazed at her nonchalant ease in the chill waters, for he had always been rather proud of his own tolerance of the crystal iciness of the North Atlantic. But now he had met someone who was more than tolerant. Always in motion, she reveled in the whirling foam, the gathering combers, the tumbling swells, and seemed oblivious to the cold. In fact, she looked perfectly at home, like a cat in a familiar living room, with a warm fire on the hearth.

"It's getting late," James said. "We really have to go back." She looked stricken.

"Go, if you must," she finally said, and there was a wistfulness to her voice. "I'm going to stay out here a little longer. Go on, don't worry about me," and she accompanied him to where the endless surge began to crest. Somehow, he felt defeated. It must have been that shimmering blue-green wetsuit, those tight leggings that went up to her waist, that were keeping her warm in those icy waters.

"See you later on the beach, Melú" he said, before turning, with some reluctance, towards shore.

"Maybe tomorrow, Jeeem," she finally replied. But a surge was gathering around him and, before he could say another word, he was swept up and hurled forward, heading back to the far-off, familiar beach.

As he rode his way home, he remembered the blue lips of his childhood when he would insist on staying in the sea beyond all bounds. For the moment, he forgot about Melú, in his eagerness to make it back to shore and dry out and gather warmth from the westering sun. There was the hiss of his first wave, then a swift crawl through to the next row, then the leap on to the back of another frothing stallion rushing towards the beach, then another interval of calm, then another foaming steed, another plunge forward, then another, and finally, the last row, where he mounted a perfect swell that carried him into the shallows from which his adventure had begun. He lay there exhausted, then stood up, unsteadily, and gazed out to sea. There was nothing to be seen but file after file of rolling surf, seven rows, and then the darker North Atlantic, stretching towards the horizon. He trudged back to his towel, dried off, lay face down, and soaked in the last of the declining mid-summer sun.

He looked for her in town that evening, walking the long main street, peering into all the restaurants, all the cafes, all the bars, but he knew it was hopeless. After a quick dinner of fried squid, he walked beyond the town to the precipice overlooking the wild Atlantic. The wind was fresh and smelled of salt and iodine, but there was nothing to be seen in the dark, except for a delicate ribbon of white unfurling down below, where the ocean met the land. He gazed out at the sea and up at the icy stars. Then he walked home along the stony path, alone in the darkness of the night.

For a week he returned every day to the same beach and every day he gazed out to sea. There were always naked children playing on the sand flats left behind by the receding tide, splashing, giggling, chasing each other in circles. There were eager dogs, a Weimaraner, a Serra da Estrela Mountain Dog, a long-haired Belgian Shepherd, a Labrador, even a clumsy Newfoundland, leaping with abandon over small waves to retrieve the sticks their masters threw. And on the beach, stretched beneath the afternoon sun, there were bikini-clad bronzed bodies, lithe and self-assured. But out beyond the breakers, there where the seventh file of frothy waves tumbled forward in eternal monotony toward the shore, there was nothing to behold. Nothing but the oceanic emptiness of the vast and beautiful sea.

DEATH BY DROWNING

It all began at sea. It was the *Groote Beer*, a student boat headed for Europe, and they all called him Zooey. It was back in the days when *Franny and Zooey* had just come out. He didn't think he was a Zooey, but he was flattered.

He met Jennifer the first day out, with Staten Island still in sight. There was the purity of her smooth skin and the glow of her untouched soul. There was also the flash of something else in her hazel eyes, something suggesting that the Virgin Mary was not the only model behind the clay of her creation. She dutifully went to Mass every day on the long transatlantic passage, and Zooey went along to make the sign of the cross and hold her hand. He had never been in love before.

The ten days were a dream. Years later, thinking back, he couldn't remember ever having fallen asleep. He remembered holding her hand, always holding her hand, even when they vomited together on the open deck, as forty-foot waves towered above them, and the ship rose almost vertical, then plunged down into a bottomless trough, as if never to rise again. He remembered the slick deck, the smell of dripping metal, the taste of salt on his lips, and, when they foolishly tried to eat, their food trays sliding up and down the table, then clattering to the floor. One other thing he remembered: somewhere near the chapel, an unhinged door banged shut, then swung open, then banged shut with the yawing of the ship, again and again. In the middle of blessing the host, the priest could not refrain from an angry gesture towards the rebellious door. Even at nineteen, Zooey could appreciate the irony.

When the North Atlantic storm passed, the pasty green of their faces gradually faded and everyone took on a ghostly drained hue. Appetites began to return and food looked good for the first time in four days. Everyone spent a lot of time on deck, lounging beneath the early summer sun. Jennifer was on a group trip with her classmates from St. Mary's. They were on their way to Lourdes, where they would be working all summer in the holy water baths. Zooey thought his college French was pretty good, but he learned a new word from Jennifer: *brancardière*. That's what she was going to be in Lourdes, carrying people on stretchers to take the holy water and be cured. She was going to assist at miracles.

They talked about books, about Europe, where they had never been, and about theater. Jennifer was a theatre major and had played Viola in *Twelfth Night*. But just then, new stuff was hitting the stage, and it was an exciting, disturbing time. They talked about *Waiting for Godot*, about *The Zoo Story*. Some of them had seen an exciting production called *The Connection*. A girl from Bennington had a Tarot deck, and they casually played their way through the cards. No one understood the complex meanings of the ancient symbols, not even the owner of the deck. When Jennifer drew Death by Drowning, she was not at all happy. Zooey himself felt uneasy and tried to comfort her. "It's a bunch of baloney, don't you think?"

After ten days of nothing but being in love, of clutching her small hand as if it were a talisman, Zooey had to leave the boat in Southampton. Jennifer and her classmates were going on to Rotterdam and from there would take a series of trains to Lourdes. "You take care, you hear me," said Jennifer. With a knapsack on his back and a guitar in his hand, Zooey marched down the gangplank and bravely waved back through his tears. He had promised to come and visit her in Lourdes.

Two months later, the summer planned by his parents was coming to an end. He had stayed with family friends near London, had visited the Tate and seen Big Ben, dutifully hitch-hiked to Stratford-upon-Avon, where he attended a performance of Hamlet, had gone on to Wales to catch a glimpse of wild ponies on Mount Snowden, then had climbed amongst the ruins of Tintagel Castle on the Cornish coast. Saying good-bye to the relative comfort of the English language, he went on to Paris, where other friends of his parents installed him in an artist's garret, heavy with the sweet smell of linseed oil and the sharper tang of turpentine. He remembered how he was shaken violently awake one morning, as tanks rolled over the cobblestones of Boulevard St. Michel to celebrate Bastille Day. He had been sure it was the end of the world. For a month, he studied six hours a day at the Sorbonne Summer School. His French had improved. Now his courses were over, he had his mini-diploma, and, at last, was ready to strike out on his own.

He said his goodbyes, consulted his brand-new Michelin, took the Metro to Port de Versailles, took a bus further south, and finally trudged, with an American flag pinned to his knapsack, to the highway heading to Blois. Two days later, exhausted and exhilarated, he found himself in Lourdes. He went to the convent where Jennifer and her classmates were housed, but was told that she was not available and he could not enter. So he wandered about, found a cheap pension, trudged up two flights of stairs, and collapsed on his springy bed. When he awoke, it was evening. He bounced out of bed, dashed down the stairs, and headed back to the convent. He pressed the buzzer, but the door did not open. A cold voice told him that no visitors could be entertained after 8 P.M. He stared at the heavy green door, but there was nothing he could do. He went and had a *biftek aux pommes frites*, a light beer, and a *crème brûlée* for dessert. Then up two flights of stairs and back to bed again.

Finally, at lunchtime the following day, when he returned to the convent, after a long wait the heavy green door opened and Jennifer slipped through and into his arms. They hugged, they held hands, they looked into each other's eyes. They went for an ice cream and huddled together, licking their cones, his vanilla, hers chocolate, and planning their escape. On Friday afternoon, they would take the train to the coast, to St. Jean de Luz, and spend the weekend at the beach.

Friday came, Jennifer appeared at their rendezvous, and off they went. At St. Jean de Luz, they found a pension right on the beach. Zooey asked for two rooms and the landlord showed him one down the hall, "C'est pour vous, monsieur," and then across the hall, another: "Et ça, c'est pour votre soeur, for your sister," he said with a complacent smile. Zooey, proud of his recently absorbed colloquial

French and even more of his moral superiority, retorted with plosive righteousness: "C'est pas ma soeur, she isn't my sister." The French landlord, a man of the world, smiled once again, but didn't say a word.

The next morning, they luxuriated on the beach, and Jennifer began to burn. Then they entered the sea. There were waves, and Jennifer was not a secure swimmer, but she believed in him and surrendered herself with utter confidence. Touched by her trust, he took her out beyond the breakers, and she went, uncomplaining, clinging to his neck. They floated together in the water, not too cold, not too warm, and Zooey wished they could have stayed out there forever. And that is how they spent their lost weekend, eating at the pension, tanning and burning on the sandy beach, floating out together beyond the waves, with Jennifer gripping him tightly by the back of his neck. It was a happy time. Zooey couldn't have asked for more.

Back at Lourdes, they were both severely chastised. Zooey protested his innocence, his honor, but the nun disarmed him with a skillful, unexpected shift away from the zone of mere morality. Tight-lipped, she told him that she didn't doubt his moral integrity. But then she added, with righteous severity, "Mais monsieur, il s'agit de sauver les apparences, it's a question of appearances." He was, in effect, banished from Lourdes. He and Jennifer parted at the Grotto of Our Lady of Lourdes. They knelt together to pray in that hallowed spot. When he opened his eyes, she was gone.

Stunned, he returned to his pension, packed his rucksack, and took the first train to Rome. There he saw the usual sights, sat on the Spanish steps, threw a coin into the fountain of Trevi, and wandered about the Colosseum. He also visited the peaceful Protestant cemetery where the ashes of Shelley, who had drowned in a storm, were buried, not far from the famous gravestone to Keats: Here lies One Whose Name was Writ in Water. By then, summer had come to its end, and Zooey, feeling both enriched and unsettled, returned to his studies in New York.

The years passed. Zooey loved islands, loved water, swam wherever and whenever he could. The Azores, Madeira, the Balearics, the Greek islands, he was always happy with the sound of noonday cicadas on the tree trunks and the roar of breaking waves or the rustle of gentle ripples. For three years, he even lived on an island in Brazil famous for its thirty-seven beaches. Jennifer, meanwhile, settled in the Midwest, far from any ocean, any sea. She married a boy from Notre Dame, she raised three boys of her own, she continued to do theater, she worked with troubled children, she went to Mass every Sunday. But except for dipping her finger to make the sign of the cross upon entering the church, water did not play a real part in her life. And they lived their separate lives, linked only by the traditional exchange of Christmas cards.

Thinking back to that precious time half a century later, Zooey realized that the landlord in St. Jean de Luz must have considered him an idiot. Now, an old man, he, too, thought he had been an idiot. But he knew that that earlier self, that amalgam of idealistic purity and vanity, was indeed what he had been, was indeed the genuine, self-assured, self-righteous, triumphant figure of his youthful self. We can grow, perhaps we can change, but we cannot change the past.

And now had come the news, after more than fifty years, that Jennifer had drowned. Swimming alone at the family summer cottage in New Hampshire, something had happened. Perhaps it had been the shock of the water, still cold in early June. Perhaps she had swum out beyond her depth, beyond her tentative belief in herself. No one could say. All they knew was that her body was seen floating face down just fifty feet beyond the dock, floating in water so still that the white birches lining the lake seemed more real in their reflected perfection than back on shore, rooted in the earth.

In any case, it was clear that she had died and that he had not been there to save her, had not been there to hold her up, as she clasped her small hands with utter faith around his neck. Suddenly came the memory of the Tarot deck on the Groote Beer and the card Jennifer had drawn. Trying to protect her, he had said, "It's a bunch of baloney, don't you think?" And he had gone on with his life. As she with hers. And when the time came, there was no one to save her. A cloud crossed the sun, and Zooey shivered. He tried to pray, but he had lost the habit long ago.

KINDNESS

Martin took great pride in his honesty. He felt that he had never lied in his life. In childhood, he had suffered much retribution for his stubborn, perhaps arrogant veracity. "How's your cherry tree?" the other kids would mock him, "How's your cherry tree, George Washington?" Then, after dancing around him in a circle, they would all run away. He couldn't explain why he refused to lie, when everyone else seemed so comfortable doing so. And surely he would have had more friends, if only he had joined the others in their barbaric tribal bickering, their vicious little lies about the fat boy down the block. But he simply couldn't do it. He could call Freddy fat, because it was true, but he couldn't say he smelled like trash, because he didn't. "Freddy Trask smells like trash! Freddy Trask smells like trash!" the neighborhood gang screamed. He couldn't stand it. Not because it was unkind, but because it was untrue. For him truth was implacably itself and could not be challenged or denied. Facts were facts. Truth was truth. Fitting in, being liked, was something else. It just couldn't be helped. That's all there was to it.

However, as he moved into adulthood, he began to be troubled by his addiction to veracity, his fierce loyalty to facts, especially when it came to romantic relationships. He could not fail to see the shadow of disappointment, of sorrow, that crossed a girlfriend's face after one of his gestures of brutal honesty. Why, if you liked someone, was it necessary to make them miserable? There was a force inside him that insisted on these attacks, attacks which part of him understood to be a rebellion against the very fabric of civility, of decency, in a word, of social life itself. Not surprisingly, despite having found a number of very fine women as romantic partners, the trajectory of his life inexorably defined itself as one of precise, curmudgeonly solitude. He couldn't remember ever having planned it that way, but as time passed, it became obvious. He would always be a bachelor.

He remembered his first real girlfriend, the lovely bangs covering her bright, broad forehead, her shining blue eyes, the perfect symmetry of her face, and her charming habit of cleaning one of her contact lenses on her tongue, while kissing him. She was tempting him with disaster; would she swallow the contact lens, would he swallow the contact lens, would it pop out and be lost in the grass or in the shrubs? Sometimes she daringly passed the contact lens to his tongue. He would be thrilled and terrified and would quickly pass it back. She had glistening white teeth and a perfect smile. She stood very straight, had a lithesome body, and could have been mistaken for a ballerina. In fact, she was a violinist. She played the Mendelsohn Concerto with a local orchestra. Utterly charming. She was descended directly from Cotton Mather. But she was not a Puritan.

She was lovely and smooth and filled with life. He bought her a blue summer frock, which turned out to be the only dress he ever bought anyone. She looked even lovelier in the frock. And lovelier later still. Everything was good. She was happy; he thought he was happy.

But one day, as he was holding forth on a concerto they both loved, she interrupted to ask: "Martin, I'm sorry, but what does mellifluous mean?"

"You don't know what mellifluous means, honey? I can't believe it. It's from the Latin for honey, you should know that, 'mel,' meaning honey. And 'fluus,' obviously meaning the flow. Latin always comes in handy, sweetie. It means flowing like honey, that's what it means, the music was flowing like honey."

"Oh, she said, and her eyes fell. "I'm sorry."

He felt a pang of sorrow for her. But after all, she was already eighteen, she was studying at a good college, shouldn't she know the simple word "mellifluous?" It wasn't logical, but he was angered by her ignorance. He took it personally. And yet he pitied her his anger.

When, with sparkling eyes, she later would say "smooth like silk" or "bright like the sun," he would cringe and feel a tightening in his heart. He would correct her, as if in passing, but they both knew it wasn't in passing at all. A year later, when graduate studies had led him half a continent away, he was not totally surprised to receive a tearful Dear John letter. He understood why she had left him. He wasn't sure he deserved the regrets she expressed. She was too kind.

Years later, in a remote provincial capital, he met a charming Brazilian woman, with an easy laugh, a good sense of humor, and a body in which she was totally at home. He considered himself lucky, at first. But then came the dénouement. He mentioned, in passing, the American astronauts who had made it to the moon. Graciosa's eyes opened wide. "The Moon," she said, as if stunned. "The moon?

Americans were on the moon?" Taking her hand, he kissed her on the cheek, then gently on her eyelids. Yes, her arms were slender, her neck long, her skin like satin, but a dagger of ice pierced his heart. Were facts that important? Did it really matter whether Americans had made it to the moon or not? Yet for him, it was now over.

At the university back home, he advanced; his publication record was stalwart, but in his personal life, even he could sense that something was amiss. He thought that perhaps fortune would shine upon him during his upcoming sabbatical. He intended to sojourn in Greece, while deepening his analysis of the role of the Apollonian in the world of the arts. Surely Nietzsche had not said it all.

After a period of research in Athens, he found himself on a Greek island of whitewashed stucco houses trimmed in blue, dropping like dominoes from the highest hillside, down to the usually quiet harbor. Every afternoon, having completed his four pages of writing, he would descend a narrow, cobbled street and take a table in the café fronting the still waters within the jetty. He would order his usual ouzo, and sit for an hour or two, content with the steady progress of his book.

Then, one day, he noticed a woman with a long, thick mane of dark hair, who seemed to scowl while smiling from within. The first time he noticed her, he nodded in a friendly way but did not approach. The next day, he asked if he might join her at her table. She responded, "Why not?" with a charming Greek accent. They shared a bottle of Retsina. Within a few days, they were lovers.

Zoey was from Crete, though she preferred to spend her time on this small island. The smell of linseed oil came from her fingers. At times her gaze would fix on the middle distance, but he could see nothing there. Her canvases were unabashed, brimming with power-ful colors, violent brush strokes, motion everywhere, no fear at all. When he spoke to her of the predominance of the Apollonian in all civilized endeavors, especially the arts, she only smiled. He himself had always tried to look as Apollonian as possible, though it troubled him when tipsy friends would suggest he offer himself as an exhibit to Madame Tussaud's in London. The same friends, at least when deep in their cups, would chide him for his almost British accent. "Just because you went to Phillips Exeter, doesn't mean you're a Brit, you know."

When Zoey showed him her canvases, he didn't know what to say. There was something lurking there, she seemed sure of herself, but it all made him feel a bit uncomfortable. He wondered if the wild colors and savage brushstrokes could somehow be tamed, domesti-cated, brought to acknowledge the overriding need for order in the universe. He was staring at canvases that almost screamed. It was as if tradition, convention, history itself had never been established. It seemed to him that her paintings were beckoning him towards a door he did not want to open. But that he could not say to her, so he would gaze at a wilderness of paint, then fall back upon the old evasion: "Very interesting." There may have been some irony in her glance, but she said nothing. He wondered about the truth, about order, and where it might be hiding in her work.

He was happy with his advancing arguments about the inevita-ble dominance, nay dominion, of the Apollonian in all human artistic endeavor. The four pages a day were adding up. He was also happy with his relationship, though he was embarrassed to find her always on top. He felt, at times, that he was like a pony being spurred across the steppes of Asia, Zoey mounted firmly on his body, riding him harder and harder, pushing, writhing to get to where she wanted to go. After their passion was spent, she would lift her body, roll to the side, and turn away, curling into herself and her dreams. He wasn't sure if, beyond the ride, he meant anything at all.

One evening, after they had returned from the cafe to her apartment, where the rich smell of linseed oil and turpentine wafted in from the adjoining studio, he was regaling her, as he often tried to do, with a meticulous account drawn from his travels. He mentioned how he had fulfilled a boyhood dream by reaching Antarctica one January, twenty years before. She had looked astonished.

"But Martin," she exclaimed, "surely it makes no sense to visit Antarctica in the middle of the winter. It must be very cold." He looked beyond her at the black windowpane of night. "Zoey," he said, through tight lips, "surely you are aware that in the Southern Hemisphere the seasons are reversed. There January is the height of summer. Surely everyone knows that?" She looked at him astonished. There was a silence, a poignant stillness in the room. "Of course," she said. "How stupid of me."

From then on, he could no longer bear to look into the dark well of her eyes. They still made love, but now even sex felt stilted, compromised, awkward. When the time came to return to Athens for more research, with some hesitation he asked if she would like to come along. She looked at him for a long moment and said: "No, Martin, I think it is better if I stay here and keep on painting. *Yia sous*, Martin. *Adio.*"

A year later, his book on the inevitable triumph of the Apollonian appeared from a University Press in the Midwest. A few critics of the old school, for the most part retired, praised his study. But there was also a torrent of criticism, sometimes tinged with ridicule, most of it coming from the West Coast. The criticism was so fierce that it generated sales, and his publisher was mildly pleased at the results. For better or for worse, Martin clearly had made his mark.

During his next sabbatical, he encountered Gudrun during a lingering excursion through Norway. He had allowed himself a lengthy detour for mere pleasure and had found her in the mountains at Geilo. She was considerably younger than he (many years had passed by then), and was ever cheerful, with rosy cheeks and a healthy, sturdy little body. She had been hitching rides during a vacation break with a girlfriend, but the girlfriend had found a young man at the youth hostel, and so she was conveniently free. Martin had a rental car from Oslo and asked her to join him. They made their way to the West Coast, visited Bergen with its waterfalls, then headed north along the fjords and the green headlands above the sea. After two nights in Tromso, where the sun never set and the townsfolk took their drinking seriously, they continued on towards Nordkapp, the northernmost point in Europe

As long as they kept moving, they were happy enough. She had a light spirit, though her body was clearly of the earth, Martin had noted. In any case, they made it to Nordkapp, where the Arctic Ocean surprised them both with its warmth. Martin collected himself and was able to explain the phenomenon. "You see, Gudrun, it's because the Gulf Stream flows up here all the way from the Caribbean, four thousand miles away." "Wow," she replied, "you must know everything, don't you?" He wasn't sure if this sturdy Norwegian girl was capable of irony. He smiled at her in a neutral fashion and left it at that.

It was that very night, there in lovely and desolate Nordkapp, in their cozy room in their small pension at the ends of the earth, that suddenly, without a thought, he said to Gudrun: "What a lovely person you are. Really. I am so lucky to have met you." And, after a pregnant pause, not knowing why, he felt compelled to add: "What a pity that such a lovely creature has such heavy ankles." She looked as if she had been shot. Without a word she gathered her toiletry, her sweater, her red bikini panties, and a few other scattered items, threw them hastily into her suitcase, bolted for the door, and, dragging the half-closed suitcase, bumped her way noisily downstairs to an empty room. He himself was surprised at his words, though, in fact, they were true. The next morning, before he was awake, she had taken the morning bus to Narvik.

As the years passed, he found himself less inclined to travel. Back home in his rather undistinguished university town, he settled down for the duration. He knew he was approaching the end of his career and really couldn't imagine what to add to his monumental tomb on the Apollonian. He felt he had said what he had to say. Most of his hair was gone and what was left had turned gray. He could still swim, of course, but his knee was bone-on-bone, and tennis had become impossible. Nonetheless, he knew he was graced with tremendous good fortune in those waning years. He had a devoted long-haired Belgian Shepherd mix, a dog who would have died for him. And he had a girlfriend who was the most solidly kind woman he had ever known. What more could he ask for? But the years were passing, and good old Shep was getting arthritic, almost unable to step down from the car.

He would walk him along the street, holding him up by his tail. His front legs were still strong, but the rear legs were rubbery. He knew what was coming, but found it impossible to confront.

Then one day, desperate over the thought of what awaited him, he blurted out the strangest declaration of love anyone had ever heard. His hand on Shep's now grizzled head, he turned to Bertha, his best companion and best support, the best woman he had ever known, and declared: "How utterly pathetic! The only person in the world I love is Shep." She said nothing, finished the dishes, then, with a light peck on the cheek, left the house and left him. He didn't think she would come back. Although what he had said was true, even he understood its cruelty. He heard a month later that she had sold her condo in town and moved back to mid-state, where she had grown up in a remote village in the mountains.

Shep died, as he had to, and now he was by himself. The years continued to pass. Mandatory retirement swept him out of his cozy office, where he had been accustomed to work till after midnight, luxuriating in the empty corridors, the quiet orderliness of the department, when no one was there. Now he lived at home, only going out in the afternoon for a walk in the nearby woods. He would sometimes leaf through his old books, many grown moldy with the years, but he rarely reread the things he had studied, the things he had taught. However, he still remembered with a certain grim affection a quote from his Anglo-Saxon class back in college days: "lif is læne: eal scæceð leoht and lif somod." "Life is fleeting: everything passes away, light and life together." Worth remembering.

As his body shrunk and the years weighed heavy, minor aches and pains increased. Then one night, the throbbing of a new pain awakened him. To his surprise, he began to think it might be time to re-examine his life. He had always assumed that by adhering to facts and to truth, he had led the good life. But in a corner of his mind, doubt apparently had been gnawing away. Nervously, he began to ask himself if he might have been wrong, if indeed there might be something more important than the truth, than being right. He began to think about kindness, a new thought for him, and was struck by how absent it had been from his arsenal of weapons. He was shocked to discover that he had never really troubled himself to consider that rather meek virtue. He began to wonder if perhaps he had been wrong all along, if perhaps he had not, after all, lived a good life. He wondered if it might be possible to make amends, to set things right, before it was too late.

And so Martin dared to call Bertha, the most loyal, trustworthy, decent, reliable woman he had ever known. He managed to reach her in her mountain village downstate. He apologized for calling, hemmed and hawed a bit, then said, in a matter-of-fact tone of voice, that he was soon going to die, and though he knew he did not deserve it, might he ask her to come and assist his passing, which, the doctors had assured him, would not be long delayed. Since she was also the most patient and long-suffering woman imaginable, she agreed to come. He breathed a sigh of relief.

And now, the time was here. The lazy woodland river below his windows flowed as it always had, but now he could feel that it was carrying him away. The crucial moment had come. He gestured to Bertha, asking her to come near. She bent over his sweating brow, his grimacing mouth, his emaciated neck, and listened. And Martin, having decided that his worship of the god of Truth had been too vehement, having decided to abandon his lifelong self-righteous, ruthless honesty, pulled himself together and, in a gravelly, broken voice, said: "Darling, everything I said, it was all a lie, it was nothing but lies. The truth is, I always loved you." With those valiant words, his last breath expended itself, his chest fell, his eyes glazed over, and a contented smile sealed his lips.

Bertha gazed at him, pressed his eyelids closed, crossed his hands on his chest, and turned back to finish the dishes. Scrubbing clean the desert bowls (yes, he had managed to down a last bit of vanilla ice cream), she chuckled to herself and couldn't help murmuring: "Poor old Marty, you can always tell when he's lying."

AUTUMNAL LOVE

Jeremiah was profoundly impractical. He could barely screw in a lightbulb. When halogen lamps came along, he wanted to cry out "Praise the Lord," though, of course, he believed in nothing. But he was deeply grateful to the meaningless universe for the new invention, since now the grace period before he had to scale his rickety stepladder to install another bulb was almost three times as long. Maps had always left him feeling bewildered, so when the GPS came on the scene, it felt like salvation. However, at times even the GPS would get it wrong and, of course, he knew that in the end neither maps nor the GPS could really save him. Nor could the copies of Modigliani women gracing his walls. He knew those women had been unable to save Modigliani or themselves, but they gave him a respite from himself and were worth the risk he took, leaning over from beyond the couch, to hammer in the nails from which to suspend their perfect bodies.

But poetry was different. As long as he kept writing, the absurdity of the universe, the perverse necessity for suffering shared by all humans and animals ("that mantis devouring the face of a bee"), was kept at bay. Writing a poem, words and images ("honey-colored death") took over, and the cruel ironies of life were nailed to the page.

("Napalm blind, raven feather smooth"). He nailed them to the page. ("I shot him through both ears/just as he bit down on a plum"). And as he hammered the keys, fixing squirming life to paper, he was also weaving a web of words ("leaves as fresh as his wife's lips") around the pain of living ("caressed by a chain saw") and it was, for the moment, encased as if in a cocoon, a cocoon of silk, ("Endless herds of bison thundering past") even if woven from the sharpest, the most piercing shards and stilettos of reality ("A peony blooming/ from the nose cavity/ of a dead child."). Words, at least while he was writing, were his salvation.

As for life, he hated it. The only moments in which a temporary suspension of defeat occurred were in driven acts of love. And so, for half a century, he pursued love, or at least sex, with dogged desperation. Sometimes there were incidents of what seemed like bliss. But mostly there were long stretches of empty desert. There had been one woman worthy of his dreams in all that meaningless unfolding of time, but when he saw her for the first time, he was struck dumb and paralyzed. When he finally shook loose from the hypnotic trance and dared to talk to her, two years had passed and she had married someone else, a safe haven, a comfortable person, someone who never said anything unexpected and never expected anything from her but dinner and washed dishes. A person who would never in a lifetime read a poem, no less write one. He had watched his one chance at transcendence fade into the fabric of ordinary day. *Carpe diem* indeed. But he had failed and could never forgive himself. He wondered what she thought about it all.

There was, however, a horrid dream that periodically visited him over the years. He would find himself suddenly flexible, like plastic man, and would bend down over himself and perform the perfect act of love. Upon awakening, he would find himself utterly abandoned, encased again in the normal, unlovely body of an ordinary man. Since each dream was impossible in its own way, he pursued women in the endless, antiseptic world of online dating. Once he met a woman who seemed enthusiastic and said she loved to suck his cock. But when he neither offered to marry her nor even asked her to move in, she disappeared from his life. Most of the women he met were less vigorously obliging.

And so the years passed, filled with anguish and solitude, but also punctuated with wondrous poems that came to him, throbbing from some other realm ("A single plum blossom/Lands without a sound/In our wine cup."). The poems were not an escape from reality. They were a wrestling match with reality, and, through words, if he wrestled them well, he would often feel that yes, he had, for the moment, bested reality, he had nailed it, pinned it to the mat ("All life howling to a halt."). It reminded him of the feeling of triumph he had had in high school as third man on the wrestling team, when, with a sudden reversal he had flipped his opponent to the floor. Only this was better.

There were quite a few good poems and even some great ones. But in the real world it was rare indeed for him to pin a woman to the mat and wrest from her body a brief semblance of bliss. And now he had come to the dreary season of life, the time when the indifference of the universe installed itself not just in his perception, but in every joint, every vein, every aching limb of his exhausted bodily frame. The end of the meaningless journey was drawing near. And now even poetry deserted him. There was nothing left to turn to except the alure of cybernetic online promises of love. And so, dragging himself from a valium-induced somnambulistic haze at 3 or 4 P.M., he would sit down at his computer and search the web for one last gasp, one last fly, a helpless creature "born between two panes of glass." But he was an aging spider, and, if by wildest chance, design did govern the universe, he was sure it no longer concerned itself with him.

But to his wonder, one day Jeremiah found her. In a dating pool called *Golden Pond* he stumbled upon a simple notice: "Woman from the countryside, recently widowed, seeking autumnal love." He responded because of the mawkish, but touchingly naive "autumnal." He wrote, she wrote back, he wrote again, she sent her address, and a week later, he and his fading old beagle limped out to the car and began the slow drive in search of a last hope.

He hated maps and he hated the GPS, but somehow, he and good old Chester, wheezing in the back, finally found themselves on a long driveway curving up a pastoral landscape towards a well-kept, freshly painted farmhouse. To one side was an open field, just beyond a row of sugar maples uncannily red in autumnal glory. In fact, the entire drive had been through the midst of hills brightly painted yellow, orange, and red, what the chamber of commerce advertised as peak fall foliage. Those emblazoned hills, with mountains rising beyond them, seemed to be crying out "Yes," in a flamboyant display of *élan vital*. Confronted, now, by the impeccable white house, his ancient heart pulsing, he thought of turning round and heading back, but was too exhausted even for cowardice. He and Chester were here and would sample what destiny, that roguish trickster, had planned for them.

And indeed, to his amazement, destiny had outdone itself. For now, at the end of his life, he encountered a lovely woman in her eighties, white hair pulled back in a ponytail, a good person, unlettered but not unkind, a woman who behaved as if she had been waiting for him her entire life. Eve welcomed them in, had a kettle boiling, slapped together a delightful smoked salmon sandwich for him and even found some attractive leftovers for Chester, who never turned down anything vaguely edible. She poured the tea, smiled and, with firm country hands, massaged Jeremiah's neck, as if she had been waiting centuries to do so. She made it all feel like a homecoming. Chester certainly had no doubts and curled up in a corner with a sigh of contentment. Jeremiah couldn't quite believe that it was real.

After two weeks, he started for home to pack up some clothes, pay some bills, put some semblance of order into his old chaotic life. But he knew he'd be coming back. It seemed as if she would be happy to keep him forever. Utterly enamored, she had hardly let him leave the bedroom during what must have been the miraculous honeymoon of her life. For him, now that the sun was setting, all his fantasies were being met. Endless desire, endless lovemaking, endless caresses, all of it coming like a gentle good-bye kiss, to a body that could feel gratitude and could house memory, but that, alas, could no longer conjure forth a triumphant physical response. Here he was enveloped in the love and bottomless desire of a kind and gentle person, an old woman filled with the yea-saying energy of youth, emerging from a lifetime of daily disappointment, who felt she had been waiting for him her entire static journey. Instead of the Kathys and Jennys of his youth, the sinewy bar girls of Saigon, the youthful sad faces of Montparnasse, outlined in mascara and rouge, he had this woman, profoundly human, profoundly ordinary, offering herself as a final, unearned, reconciliation with things as they are. How ironic that he no longer had the strength to turn it all into a poem.

Yes, he thought, with a sigh, as he drove away, gazing out the window at fading leaves falling, twirling down to merge with the mottled brown carpet of previous seasons. Yes, this was the road he had traveled by, and he had come at the right time. The only time. Would it be so bad, after all, to close down his anguished poetic solitude and settle now for the remains of mere reality?

IN THE YEAR OF THE PLAGUE, 2020

Long tresses of golden hair floated like a wild cloud of gossamer in her wake. Her feet seemed to barely touch the ground. She ran a different configuration of trails through the woods each day, and she seemed so concentrated on her training that she hardly noticed Peter's presence. But whenever he took his salutary hour-long stroll through the pleasant twists and turns of the byways in the woodland near his home, he would catch glimpses of her, flitting through the trees, passing swiftly through the gently gathering dusk. When her path happened to pass not far from him, Peter would give her a civil nod of the head, a small acknowledgment between the only two figures sharing the twilit forest traces toward the close of day. He could not tell in the dim light if she returned his courtesy. But he could see that she was not wearing the face mask strongly recommended by the authorities in these troubled times. Peter, a good citizen, always put on his face mask when encountering another human being.

Peter liked taking his therapeutic walks just as dusk began to gather because at that late hour there was less chance of bumping into other people, an occurrence to be avoided by a vulnerable man in his late seventies. He also welcomed the increased possibility of catching a glimpse of an occasional deer or perhaps even a fox during the extended June twilight. Once he surprised a lone buck that snorted its astonishment, before leaping out of sight. Another time, he caught sight of a group of four deer browsing a peaceful meadow just beyond the thicket through which he was passing. He stopped to watch, and the deer stood frozen, watching him. Only when he began to walk again did they signal alarm, flashing their white tails in the air, as they quickly bounded off together.

It was 2020, the first year of the modern plague that had cast a pall over the earth. Country after country had fallen ill and normalcy was a dream of the past. Neither scientists nor politicians knew what to do and no one could say when, if ever, the pandemic would disappear. A blanket of gloom enveloped the globe and even the sanguine were plagued with insomnia. In the United States, still in the 21st century a country of brash, unthinking teenagers and energetic yahoos, things were worse than anywhere else. One third of worldwide pandemic cases had blossomed in that single country. It had already lost more than double the casualties of the infamous Vietnam War.

However, for Peter, the crisis was not so unpleasant. He was elderly, a retired professor, and a lifelong bachelor. In a word, aloneness was not new for him. He listened to the news reports and resigned himself quite willingly to a prolonged, voluntary social isolation. It wasn't a major change after all. He felt this crisis was, in fact, a kind of invitation to broaden his normal practices, and he accepted the invitation. He listened to his old recordings of Casals, Rostropovich, Menuhin, Heifetz, Stern, and Richter. Bach's six Cello Suites seemed best to fill the present silence. He also decided it was time to reread the classics, from *The Odyssey* to *Middlemarch*, and so he settled into his old leather armchair and sank into the comforting otherness and familiarity of those imagined worlds. He was content in the company of wily Odysseus and sage Penelope, acutely aware that no such creatures would intrude upon the quiet dissolution of his own small tale.

Peter's only adventure, in fact, beyond the confines of his home, was that one-hour daily walk in the nearby wood. He felt that this regular outing was important for his physical and mental health. The stillness of the forest, the occasional chirping of a thrush or cardinal, the tiny frogs hopping across the path, were deeply comforting, suggesting that, after all, life does go on, at least in the world of nature. And so, every afternoon, just before the sun sank from sight, he would head for the woods and, using a new pair of trekking sticks to take weight from his arthritic knees, would follow the meander of foot paths carpeted with pine needles and pinecones. He loved the thickening gloam just after sunset and was happy to have the woods to himself.

However, he did notice, nearly every day, that same slender woman, with those long locks of golden hair, always clad in black, swiftly passing along the twilit trails as he himself, leaning heavily on his trekking poles, would make his way, slowly and carefully, along the narrow tracks and traces scattered throughout the woods. He would see her in the distance, flickering along in the last rays of the setting sun that sliced between the stolid tree trunks, apparently unaffected by the uphill stretches, always gliding forward, always at the same unhurried, yet steady pace. Peter would reach for his mask, but the runner, slender legs in black tights, a tank top clinging to her breasts, would quickly disappear from sight, like any other woodland creature, and the mask would prove superfluous.

As the weeks passed, Peter grew accustomed to her fugitive presence in the network of forest trails that only they seemed to share. Once in a while, her trajectory would come close to his own, and Peter would immediately put on his face mask, while giving her a friendly, if somewhat distant, wave. During these brief but closer encounters, he made out a broad white brow and dark eyes, sunken in shadow. Her body was that of an athlete, and he assumed she was young, but, in fact, from what little he saw of her face, she could have been almost any age at all. She always passed by at a swift pace, but he never heard the sound of labored breathing. One evening he had startled a red squirrel that clung to its branch and stared at him with trembling intensity. But strangely enough, as the runner glided by, the red squirrel didn't give her a glance. It was as if, for him, she hadn't been there at all.

On his strolls, Peter sometimes thought of Odysseus and his own mixed feelings for that ancient hero. In the end, he felt he could only admire that shifty strategist, that cunning plotter and planner, for one thing. And that was the rejection of Nausicaa's offer of marriage. Nausicaa, obviously, was as lovely, high-born, and wise as his wife Penelope, and she was conveniently twenty years younger. Had the hero accepted the generous suggestions of her parents and herself, he would have found himself the new king of a new kingdom, with a charming, deeply intelligent bride of seventeen. It would have been as if the twenty years of war in Troy had never happened. But he rejects this offer and insists on returning to his own kingdom and his own wife, Penelope, now a middle-aged woman with, like himself, wrinkles on her brow. This decision impressed Peter, who was not sure he would have been able to embrace reality at the price of such an attractive alternative.

Shifting from Odysseus to himself, Peter would at times wander amongst memories of his own youthful affairs, his adventures in the long-lost world of Eros. He remembered the excitement of the first sighting, the intense pursuit, the impassioned chase, the sometimes-ecstatic conclusion. He remembered with embarrassment how he had kept an alphabetical list of names, of lovely conquests: Anna, Barbara, Clarissa, Eloise, Franny, Georgiana, Harriet, Inez, Jennifer, Karina, Lisa, Marianne, all the way through Quintard, the Southern Belle, Xenia, the Russian poet, and Zoe, the Greek exchange student, with her enormous dark eyes. How callow he had been. What shameful practices does the frenzy of youth propel us towards. He still wondered, however, why there had been no Daphne, Dahlia, Dorothy, Dolores, Diane, or Dionysia on his childish checklist. Not to mention Desirée. He had never met a Desirée. Well, in any case, all that foolishness was now a thing of the past. Now he could bask in the late sun of books, music, and these delightful afternoon strolls through the natural world.

And so the first year of the plague continued. Various countries, desperate for normalcy, would drop their quarantines, their social isolation, their meticulous precautions. And then the plague would gather force once again. None of this had any effect on Peter, who continued reading his way through the Greeks, delighting especially in their overpowering and monumental women. Their very names still stirred his blood: Clytemnestra, Antigone, Medea. He felt a chill go down his spine. Those women were something to be reckoned with. They towered over their men. They were no man's conquest.

And, of course, he continued his daily visits to the woodlands. And there, as always, he would see the lithe and implacable athlete on her endless training run. It seemed that now their routes were tending to draw nearer to each other. He wondered if they would ever speak, if he might even learn her name. Could she turn out to be, at this late date, the Desirée he had never met, he mused, with an ironic little grin?

Then there came a day when, quite unexpectedly, the stranger stopped in the middle of her effortless stride and looked at him. For the first time, he gazed into her eyes that echoed like a starless night. She slowly drew closer, and he became aware of a heavy odor, a mixture of humus, low tide, and something sweet and mysterious. As always, she wore no mask, and her lips were swollen and bright red. There was no trace of lipstick. She drew closer and he stood there paralyzed. She came within arm's length, and he shuddered. Reaching out, she gently, but firmly, like a nurse, removed his N95 Coronavirus Face Mask. She let it drop to the forest floor. She spread wide her naked arms but never said a word. Peter was mesmerized. He hadn't been with a woman in many years. He had been convinced that Eros was completely behind him. After all, he was an old man, only able to follow the forest paths thanks to his new set of trekking poles. But as she drew even closer, his poles fell, useless, to the ground, and he found himself leaning into her embrace. She encircled him with her naked arms and drew him closer to her strangely ageless, alien, yet familiar face. She gently brushed her swollen lips against his thin and withered mouth. She softly licked his dry and trembling lips with her pink tongue, then gently slid it between his lips. When, like a burrowing animal, it slipped its way toward his tongue and touched it on the tip, he felt a jolt of lightning pass like a spasm through his body. He knew this was the consummation of his life. That was all he knew.

The next morning, a teenager without a mask, riding by on his mountain bike, came across the old man's body beside the trail. Two trekking poles and an N95 face mask were lying on the pine needles and leaf litter beside him. The youngster, of course, had his I-phone with him, so he called 911. They were sending an ambulance, but insisted he stay by the body until the paramedics arrived. It felt weird, but he stayed. As soon as they came and confirmed his name and phone number, he jumped on his bike and rode off. The paramedics had a long trail to climb with the body on the stretcher, but they were grateful that the withered old man didn't weigh much. After half an hour, they got the body into the ambulance and brought it back to the regional hospital. They had seen many bodies these last two months.

The tests came back the next day. One doctor, summarizing the results, declared that the man had died from Covid-19. A colleague, examining the same results from the lab, suggested there was no clear indication that coronavirus had been the cause of death. The supervisor came bustling by, leafed through the paperwork, and declared the final verdict on the lab report: inconclusive.

Down in the hospital morgue, a young attendant was about to slide the cadaver back into its drawer. "Poor guy," he said to himself, "look how shriveled his body is." Then he added, reflectively, "Well, at least he died in the woods, not in this damned place." And with that final benediction, clicking the drawer shut on the old man, he turned to another wrinkled old body on an adjacent slab. "I wonder how long this pandemic's gonna last," he mused. But for the time being at least, it was not really his problem. He was young, strong, healthy, and it was mostly the old who were dying.

A TOUCH OF UNEXPECTED GRACE

It was thirty-three years ago, when they both were young. After the dancing had ended and the bar was closing down, they drove to the wind-swept open beach where, hand in hand, they climbed the rocks jutting out into the ocean. Was there a moon or was it just the stars? He couldn't remember, but there had been enough light for them to see a lone dolphin suddenly flash through the dark water, then disappear, leaving a sparkling trail of phosphorescence in its wake. An apparition, a message from a benevolent universe. He pulled her close against the nighttime chill. How lucky they had been to see that emissary. They exchanged a kiss.

Then they went to his bungalow on the lagoon. She, already in bed, he, brushing his teeth. Then, snapping off the bathroom light, he turned eagerly for the bed. She was lying there, a lovely dark offering beneath the white sheet. He was about to slip in beside her when he noticed that she looked frozen, that her teeth were chattering.

"Are you feeling sick, Claudia?" he asked. She shook her head.

"Is it too cold, should I get a blanket?" Again, she shook her head.

"Well, what's wrong, honey?" he persisted. She shook her head again, mouth clamped shut.

"Oh, no, I can't believe it. You're not a virgin, sweetie, are you?" Her eyes grew wide as she nodded tragic affirmation. He stood stunned, a few feet from the bed. She was educated, articulate, a social worker, a sexy dancer, filled with grace. She was twenty-six and Brazilian. It had never entered his head. "Here, Claudia, let me help you get dressed," he said, with an embarrassed briskness, holding out her smooth, white skirt. "Oh, sweetie." He didn't know what else to say. In silence, he helped her get back into her clothes, walked her out to his Karmann-Ghia, and drove her to the young ladies' residence in town. He squeezed her hand, those long, delicate fingers, those innocent fingernails, gave her a gentle kiss on her satin-smooth cheek, then walked around to open the door. She got out, they exchanged another kiss, and, seeming relieved, she hurried into the silent ladies' residence.

He had understood, immediately, the significance of her condition. She was middle-class, she was proper, and traditional Brazil, despite discos, booze, and marijuana, was still lingering on. If he had accepted her sacrifice and then not married her, her life here in the provinces would have been ruined. She was both idealistic and practical and had already been working to help the impoverished remnants of indigenous tribes who suffered from the invasion of their lands. Her goodness was deeply entwined with her country's history and its current sufferings. He couldn't imagine her living in his own brutally materialistic, utterly commercialized country, where money was everything. But he already knew he wouldn't be able to stay here, to adjust to her country, with its easy flow, its insouciance, imprecision, unreliability, and its casual macho hedonism, linked to a deeply embedded double standard. So, the moment she nodded her head, he knew he could not sleep with her. He may have been frustrated, but he wasn't angry. There had been no deception, just a serious misunderstanding. In any case, there was no point in going on.

And now, after all that time, twenty pounds heavier, his remaining hair gone grey, James was back in her city as a distinguished guest lecturer, wondering what had happened to the lovely Claudia, so sexy and so good. He made a few inquiries and discovered that she had married a left-leaning politician and former athlete. Her husband had become mayor of the city just after the dictatorship finally ceded power. But many years later, apparently, there had been a divorce, under murky circumstances. That's all they would tell him. But then someone came up with a phone number, and he thought he might at least have a chat with the past. So he called.

And now she was taking him on a little tour, as they headed towards the interior, the unfamiliar backlands of the state. It was, however, a strange time of year to be a tourist, for the fallow fields were coated with a thin layer of frost, almost unknown in Brazil. They both wore insulated winter jackets. She drove and talked. She told him, balancing embarrassment and irony, of her last thirty years: the happy beginning, her husband's political success as he rose from wrestling star to communist mayor of a provincial capital, the long hours at work, the two children gracing their marriage, the husband's exhaustion when he would finally come home, the dwindling away of their sexual relationship, the growing of the two boys, the adjustments she made to her husband's increasing absence and his replacement of affection with politeness; and then, after more than twenty-five years of what seemed a normal, if not deeply romantic, marriage, the unknown phone number that appeared on the cell phone he had left on the table at lunchtime. And that had explained it all.

"Can you believe it, Jimmy?" she said. "I called the number, and a woman's voice, filled with joy, answered the phone. I hung up. You know who it was, Jimmy? It was his girlfriend from thirty years ago. He had been in love with her, but she had married someone else, someone with more money. Frustrated and ashamed, he proposed to me on the rebound, as we say, and I foolishly accepted. Well, turns out that after a week, she realized she had made a big mistake. She called him up and said that, after all, he was the one she really loved. So, without a word, he went back to her. Both of them were locked into their marriages, but she was the love of his life. And that was where his passion flowed for the next thirty years. I had no idea. I stayed home, raised the kids, and pitied my husband for his long hours at the mayor's office. And that's the story of my life," she concluded, with a little laugh.

Time had not been kind to Claudia. Her long, slim fingers were now puffy with age, and, although she had managed to soap and pull off her wedding band after the debacle, the many other rings looked as if they were embedded in her flesh for the duration. Her slender neck was swollen with the years. Her flat stomach sagged, her waist was bordered now by a roll of fat. Her face had thickened and looked care-worn. But her eyes had not changed: chestnut brown, full of light, humor, irony, and goodness. She was still Claudia, and, having accumulated the inevitable losses of a lifetime, his first love to drowning, another love to cancer, his faithful Golden Retriever to old age, and finally his mother, who he thought would live forever since she had been there from the beginning, with all that had vanished, he felt fortunate to have found her again. As for the body housing the soul, he knew about that. He hadn't looked in a mirror for years.

It was after midnight when they pulled into a quiet, cold town in a rural valley. Even in the dark, they could see the darker black of the mountains rising above them. They had to ring the outside bell, for no one was in attendance, and the door was locked. After several minutes, a sleepy man appeared and opened the door. They went to the desk, and it was only then that James discovered Claudia's intentions. "Quarto de casal," she said in a deep, confident voice, like someone who had said that countless times before. So now, after thirty-three years, they were going to consummate what usually is consummated in one's youth. James felt nervous, but he also felt he was in the presence of an old friend.

They trudged upstairs with their overnight bags. He favored his left knee, already bone-on-bone. He heard her wince when she shifted her day bag. Even that light weight, it seemed, was enough to provoke the rheumatism in her wrist. They entered an ordinary room with white walls, an overhead light, and a picture of the Sacred Heart of Jesus. There was also a sagging double bed. They took off their winter jackets, hung them up, and took turns in the bathroom. As he brushed his teeth, he remembered the other time in his bungalow long ago, just before discovering Claudia's virginity. This time there was no virgin in the room, just old age. The insistence of youth, hormonal, needy, exigent, was gone. He stood in the room filled with doubt, unsure what to say, how to act. Did their bodies know what they wanted to do? Did *they* know what they wanted to do? Wasn't it too late for eros?

They turned their backs to each other as they slipped into sweats, the modern substitute for pajamas. They stretched out in the bed, under three layers of blankets, and he switched off the light. After their fumbling efforts ended, she gave an embarrassed laugh and said in her husky voice: "I'm sorry. I'm really sorry. The truth is I'm a virgin all over again. It's been years since my husband slept with me, I really don't remember how to do this." "Don't worry," he mumbled, "don't worry," as he caressed her arm and gave her a comforting hug. At least we are friends, good old friends, fellow human beings, he thought, as they drifted from embarrassment into sleep.

He awoke shortly before dawn and lay still, thinking. Here was this good creature, Claudia, once so beautiful, so slender, so utterly charming in her looks and ways, and now, how transformed by cynical time. He reached for her pudgy hand in the dark and held it. And as he did so, he began to feel that perhaps this woman, who had suffered and aged, who had lost her youth and her promise, who had discovered that her thirty-year marriage had been an illusion, was quietly and deeply desirable, after all. He did not feel the inexorable rising of passion as in youth. Instead, he felt a sympathy, an understanding, a compassion for her. After all, they both had aged, they both had lost their youth, they both were well along the road to vanishing. And here they lay, side by side in the dark, linked by a common fate. He felt pity growing in him, pity for her, for himself, for all flesh and its fading power. Slowly, gently, he slipped back into her half-sleeping body, and this time they traveled together smoothly and naturally, two ephemeral creatures abandoned by the cravings of youth, facing together the inevitable. As the indifferent beauty of morning's first grey touch filtered into their room, he was flooded by the pathos of the human condition, the vanity of the animal self and its ever-aspiring soul, its utter helplessness beneath the arc of mortality. And there rose within him, like the freshness of a mountain spring, a love limpid and deeper than youthful desire.

How happy he was that he and Claudia had taken this brief journey to the interior. Even if life would draw him inexorably back to New York next week and, as way leads on to way, he might never see her again, he would carry with him always this glimpse of possibility, of something unforeseen and bewildering, this touch of unexpected grace.

ACKNOWLEDGEMENTS

I would like to thank the editors of Open Ends Press for their willingness to bring this collection, largely of misadventures, to the light of day. In addition, I would like to thank the editors of the following magazines that published many of these ironic excursions into nuanced failure:

American Chess Magazine

Bitter Oleander

Bloom

Gavea-Brown

Kelp

Lasso

Latin American Literary Review

Mediterranean Poetry

Offcourse

Stockholm Review

And special thanks, of course, to Russell Enterprises, the publisher of an earlier book of chess memories and inventions: *The Last Ruy Lopez: Tales from the Royal Game,* from which six of these stories were drawn.

ABOUT THE AUTHOR

Alexis Levitin has published fifty-two books of translations, including Clarice Lispector's *Soulstorm* and Eugenio de Andrade's *Forbidden Words*, both from New Directions. He is the recipient of two National Endowment for the Arts translation awards, has held Fulbright positions in Portugal, Brazil, and Ecuador, and has been a translation resident at Banff, Canada, Straelen, Germany (twice), and the Rockefeller Foundation Center at Bellagio, Italy. During the fear-tinged isolation of the pandemic, he began writing his own stories. So far, nearly seventy of them have appeared in magazines in the USA, England, Norway, Sweden, Spain, Italy, and Turkey. A collection of chess memories and inventions, *The Last Ruy Lopez: Tales from the Royal Game,* was published in 2023 by Russell Enterprises.